DARK

DARK TIMES

DANIEL KRAMB

December 2008

This was war.

That much was clear. Nothing else could explain the situation: broken glass, a smashed sink, half a window frame. Nothing else could explain the debris, or the dust, which, by now, was all around him.

Jonathan tripped again.

Was this it, finally?

The darkness only allowed glimpses; here, now, then gone: piles of rubble. Large blocks of concrete. Shredded plastic sheets and wooden boards with long nails coming out.

Was this it?

Jonathan grabbed for a hold, but whatever was hanging from up there simply gave way, bringing down crumbling fragments and grey ashes and more and more of the fine dust that was biting lungs that still only wanted a cigarette.

He was alive.

That much was clear; and he was determined to go on, despite the darkness and despite the dirt. Determined to cling to whatever was left, and to whatever would be left, after this.

He coughed.

Whatever that was; Jonathan stumbled past another sink, almost intact this time, and over splinters of glass, gnashing at his shoes, and avoided another pile and walked on, until he reached a coarse stone wall, which provided some hold, if only for a minute.

If only for now, breathing in and out:

Everything was under control.

In and out:

Everything would become clear.

He turned around.

All he had to do was to do what he always did and that was to keep going.

He looked up.

All he had to do was to find out, where, for Christ's sake, the blonde-haired girl had come from, now standing right in front of him.

Grinning.

Assuring him that he wasn't alone. That he wasn't lost, after all, but was perfectly fine, because despite the darkness, the dirt and the dust, there was only one question:

Did he fancy her?

That was the state; Jonathan pinched his bleary eyes to zoom in, but the girl had already turned into a guy who had neither hair nor a shirt, but was grinning just as much.

If this really was what it seemed to be, the whole sorry situation coming to an end, finally, then why the hell was everyone smiling?

Jonathan jerked his head to the left.

And to the right.

And to the left again, but she was gone and so was the guy, which left Jonathan with no other choice but to stumble on, over ceramic splinters and burnt-out remains.

Towards a sense of place.

Towards a sense of time.

Towards a sense of self; one messy mind streaming forward, as minds tend to do, in here as everywhere, towards a little more clarity.

Jonathan kicked away an empty bucket.

Towards a little more truth.

Jonathan swallowed.

Was this the big one, finally, or was he suffering through yet another promise, not to become what it had to become, eventually, his clenched fist hurled at whatever was announcing itself, only to disappear again, terrible images flickering up and down and up again?

Never staying long enough to reassure him.

Jonathan tripped again.

His fist loosened.

His fingers touched something cold.

He looked up.

This was different; Jonathan started banging, teeth clenched, against whatever was hissing that the foreshadowing was over, once and for all, and kept banging, his flat hand against the cold metal, in a rhythm he didn't choose, as if directed, for just a moment.

As if steered?

Jonathan pushed, but nothing moved.

As if...

Jonathan allowed his head to sink against the cold metal and started shaking it, slowly.

If this city was coming to an end, he was prepared.

He pushed again.

If this city was coming to an end, Jonathan would have to come to an end too.

This was London.

This was all he had; he pushed again and then the door gave way, all of a sudden, and Jonathan tripped over the sill and was blinded.

"You know doors have handles you can push down?"

Jonathan squinted.

Around him, there were noises, but not those of war.

He rubbed his eyes.

Around him, there was bright daylight, and that was a pretty good indication as to what was going on, all of a sudden.

"You're right?"

Jonathan tried to open his dry mouth.

He still had his legs.

He still had his arms.

"Yeah..." he mumbled, and:

"What time is it?"

Everything would be fine.

All around him, fellow survivors were resting their tired heads on other people's laps.

Everything would be good.

"Half ten, mate," someone said.

Jonathan smiled a little, because that was all he needed to know, really.

He coughed.

Because, now that a cold winter wind was returning a clearer vision, this was just the way it had been a hundred times before, weak-legged stumbling out of a war zone and into another day and Jonathan stepped, carefully, over empty cans of Red Stripe and shoes without owners and small bottles of water and shared packs of tobacco and towards whatever would come next.

"Are we slightly disoriented there?"

Jonathan stepped over bodies.

"Yeah, yeah..."

Jonathan walked away from this front line, because that was the only way, in this particular situation in Shoreditch, East London, as in any situation.

"Yeah, yeah..."

Jonathan dumped the vaguest sense of a connection for another night, another story:

Jonathan left everything behind.

On his left, the guy without hair or a shirt was no longer grinning, but sleeping, and so was the blonde-haired girl, her small breasts huddled against his naked flesh.

Jonathan did fancy her.

But it was too late now.

"Let's go have breakfast somewhere," someone said behind him, but someone else answered:

"Let's have another beer."

But Jonathan continued to limp away, down a narrow pathway he now remembered, vaguely, from a hundred years ago, even though it had only been last night that he had taken it in the opposite direction, striding, anticipation-filled, at about three times the speed he was managing now.

"Let's smoke another spliff," someone said.

But Jonathan kept going

As intended, he was listening to the only voice that could be trusted, on every corner, at every junction:

"Yeah, yeah..."

As intended, there was no one to consider, ask or wait for, but Jonathan:

Fully in charge.

"Let's have some sex," someone said, but Jonathan left them behind the way he had to.

"Yeah, yeah..."

There was only himself, on this pathway, as in life:

Moving, but without a destination.

Numb beats were once again coming from the disused warehouse that had so nicely trapped him all night, another Friday taken off to drink with a Thursday crowd, but Jonathan pushed the massive black metal gate in front of him and stepped onto a pavement that delivered the final bit of reassurance he still needed:

This was London, unscathed.

He started smiling.

This was the 149, opening doors and closing doors and rushing off, Edmonton-bound, as the smell of Vietnamese food met the comforting stink of a hundred exhausts and the sweat from a drowsy drifter, who was clutching the breakfast beer Jonathan needed so desperately.

He had done it again.

That much was clear.

Jonathan leaned against the poster-besmeared wall behind him and started slithering down, with legs that were simply giving way and with nothing else objecting. On the other side of Kingsland Road, a car started honking aggressively at whatever was in its way, but that noise and the siren that was approaching and the drifter's random slur merely blended into the comforting lullaby the sound of this city had long become.

Jonathan reached the ground.

Everything was perfectly fine.

He had survived another war; everything was exactly the way it should be.

Jonathan closed his eyes.

As if to say welcome, the staff ID reader beeped as Sarah held her pass against it.

As if to say that everything was okay.

On her mobile, in her other hand, boyfriend Peter said, with excitement in every syllable:

"Anyway, I have such amazing news. Can you talk?"

And, without waiting for an answer:

"You don't even know how happy I am, Sarah."

Sarah pushed the door that led to the national newspaper's open plan office, where the fluorescent light was shining as if to say welcome, once again, to this world, neatly arranged and cleaned over night, screen for screen for screen.

Desk for desk.

Row for row for row for row.

"Great, what's the news?"

Sarah took her place in the far corner.

She placed her paper cup of coffee shop coffee on the table and her winter jacket over her chair and slumped down, pressed the button that booted her computer and moved her keyboard in position.

She leaned back.

Ready to do what was expected of her.

"Maybe I should tell you tonight, actually. I'll bring another bottle of wine and we'll celebrate, okay?"

"If you prefer, but, hey I –"

"Sorry, Sarah, there's just…I'll call you back, okay?"

Someone a little more important.

"Sure, yeah."

Someone worth hanging up for, a sudden expectation expressed and met, because performance was constant, slips deadly. Mistakes could not be excused, because, for better or worse, that was how the future was made: impression by impression. Modest promotion by modest promotion, one opportunity at the time.

They both knew that.

Amazing news?

Sarah pushed her back against the rest of her chair; she was still cold from a journey that was far too familiar to occupy this precious space, but did, nevertheless, just because her computer needed too long to cooperate.

As every morning:

She had waited where the office shuttle stopped, picking up those with leather bags and tennis racquets, with early morning thoughts and their hair still wet.

She had grabbed the grey straps of the 149, where it had been briefcases against babies, with those running the show pushing those making it possible into their place, claiming their rightful position as the ones moving things, responsibility written all over their shiny, nicely groomed faces:

Moving share prices.

Moving files around the office.

Moving the world, not just moving prams, as they barked into smart phones:

"No, we can't postpone this until next week," and:

"Ex-cuse me."

Was she becoming more like Stoke Newington, or was Stoke Newington becoming more like her?

She blew at her coffee.

As for five years, she had travelled down the High Street without reading, thinking, talking, as the well-known scenes had passed: the bright kebab places, already putting big lumps of meat onto sticks, and the cafés, serving lattes to creative types with jobs, but no offices, and the last remaining caffs, serving weak tea to those that had neither.

Sarah moved her mouse.

As usual, she had secured a seat somewhere close to Dalston Junction, where the white cranes had hailed the redevelopment, slickly designed and secured by gates: homes for the likes of her, being shuffled, once again, through the same streets.

The same junctions.

The same turns.

Towards the same staff ID reader that had only waited to make its reassuring sound...

And why the hell was she even thinking about this again?

Everything was just fine.

Everything was perfectly okay; Sarah clicked to scan the flurry of press releases that were waiting every time she opened her inbox, sent late the other night in a vain hope that early in the morning even Sarah was happy to read what no one needed to know; she started deleting.

"Thinking outside of the box for you," one said.

Whatever that meant.

Sarah had a few careful sips towards the precious reaction the day's first coffee still caused inside her head, and allowed the drifting:

A life, a box.

It made sense, didn't it?

Especially on a Friday morning like this, when the walls could not be overlooked.

When the situation was painfully obvious, this office and her flat and nothing in-between.

When the clearly defined borders of her existence were marked with bright yellow signs that warned her not to cross.

It made perfect sense:

Her life, a box and on a Friday morning like this, it was as if a daunting squad of soldiers was guarding it, telling her without moving their lips: not to move. On mornings like this,

Sarah could see them gloating as they shielded her life, her world, her universe, and shouted without saying a thing:

Not to dare.

Sarah hugged her coffee cup from both sides.

That was the deal, wasn't it?

Once you had allowed the soldiers to take their positions, a hundred eyes on constant alert, you couldn't even come close to the border any longer. You couldn't even dream about trying. Once you had come this far, that was that.

When had she allowed them to pick up those guns?

Sarah rushed up.

Her phone displayed the name of the magazine's commissioning editor, who was only a month in his job, because, in here, everyone constantly moved, keeping things fresh and keeping everyone longing for the next move and keeping everyone equally dissatisfied, as they plotted the kind of moves Sarah was expected to plot as well.

It was called career.

"Sarah speaking," she said.

"Sarah, hi, I was wondering if you could do me a favour?"

Well.

"Sure," she said, because if you didn't play by the rules, you lost. It was that simple.

"What can I do for you?" she said.

"You know the new slot we have about ordinary people, towards the end of the Saturday magazine?"

"I've seen it, yes."

Which was a semi-lie, but that was what office life consisted of, basically.

"Great. We have an interview lined up for today, but no one to do it. Could you step in?"

"Sure," she said and stared at her screensaver, which was displaying, by a not-to-be-changed default, the same name and logo that decorated the canteen plate still lying on her desk from late last night.

"Great, I'll send the stuff through straight away."

You are your employer.

You are your standard size business card.

You are your extension line.

"Great."

"Thanks."

"Sure."

Sarah had another sip from her coffee; she would get this distraction from her to-do list out of the way straight away and move on quickly, putting these unhelpful thoughts where they were best kept, and make this Friday pass and touch out and ask the 149 to shuffle her towards boyfriend Peter and his amazing news.

She opened the email as it arrived:

"Here's the guy's number. He refuses to give up the hunt for his dream job. You know the type. Just ask the questions below. And please don't waste too much time on it."

Sarah shook her head; refusing to give up the hunt for your dream job?

She smiled, picked up the phone and mumbled:

"Wait until you get it."

"For fuck's sake," Lizzie screamed and grabbed the towel holder in front of her.

"Who broke that stupid toilet seat again?"

But there was no answer.

She tried not to touch the wobbly, piss-stained piece of plastic underneath her. Going to the toilet in this flatshare was like going to the shit-covered toilet of a music festival, only worse, and, secretly, Lizzie was sick of it.

"Hello?"

Secretly, Lizzie couldn't see them anymore, the smelly cellars and dingy boxes she spent her time in, with stomach-turning kitchens and damp bedrooms, with no windows, and with corridors full of useless clutter and mice and rats and vermin all over the place.

"Anyone?"

But this was the life she chose to live, a stinky flatshare above Ridley Road Market, Dalston, because the arrangement was like that, wasn't it?

You chose.

To tramp, bundle in hand, from one dump to the next, because flats and neighbourhoods and cities were like friends, or anything, and that meant:

It was up to you.

To swap Hoxton for Homerton and leave Lower Clapton for a year in London Fields, jumping back and forth between the postcodes that made up the north-eastern stretch of madness Lizzie called home.

She almost slipped.

"Fuck."

This was the life she chose to live, but now Christmas wasn't far and that meant explaining this choice to those that didn't understand.

Lizzie flushed.

She washed her hands without soap, because there was no soap and dried her hands on her leggings, because there was no towel, and stepped into the corridor.

"Think it was Pedro," Amanda said from the kitchen.

Lizzie entered.

"Then why isn't the idiot fixing it?"

But Amanda, flicking through Lizzie's ID magazine, said:

"Going out tonight?"

Because that was the question everyone in this flatshare asked, even though everyone in this flatshare knew perfectly well that the answer was predetermined:

"Yes, shit," Lizzie said, and:

"What day is it?"

"It's Friday, sweetheart," Amanda said, throwing her arms into the air in a gesture of fake jubilation.

"It's the weekend!"

As if the weekend made any difference.

"Shit, yeah, I need to call someone," and:

"You?"

"Private view on Vyner," Amanda said without looking up.

"Haven't got the details."

"Right, if you see Pedro, tell him I'll shoot him."

"Will do."

Lizzie entered her share of the flat, which was a mattress found on Shacklewell Lane and a wardrobe found on Graham Road, and nothing else.

She grabbed her phone to arrange a catch-up, even though there was nothing to catch up on.

Lizzie dialled.

Even though there was no movement other than the one from up here to The George.

From Visions to The Boudoir and vice versa.

From her mattress to the loo to the kitchen sink and back, staring out of a window that had too many cracks to prevent the winter cold from carrying in the biting smell of the foul fish from the market below, where they were at it already, pound a bowl, pound a bowl.

Lizzie said:

"Hey, still up for tonight then?"

"Sure. Seven still good?"

It was always seven and it was always The Royal Oak on Columbia Road, which meant meeting in the middle, of sorts. It was always a shared bottle of wine and Lizzie talking about trying and Claire talking about not even trying anymore.

"Yep, cool."

Sweet Claire, who had never been made for this: far too organised and not nearly free-thinking enough. Still doing whatever shitty sales job she had accepted after university.

"Great, see you there."

But at least she made the effort, despite this being London, where advance planning was required, appointments needed. Where farewell tears were as intimate as a handshake and time flew, even though nothing ever happened.

At least not for Lizzie.

"Want anything from the shop?" Amanda half-screamed from the corridor.

Lizzie let her mobile fall onto her mattress. She still had time before she would have to board the 149, all shades of human life squeezed next to each other.

"Can I have a pack of Golden Virginia?"

Where things wouldn't be too busy at this time; the working world going the other way, the drinking world not quite going to Shoreditch yet.

"Most certainly not."

"Get lost then."

The working world, streaming out, longing for couches. Longing for relief.

"Want Rizzlas too?"

The lunching classes, whose only joy in life was lunch, one hour every day, and who, briefcases in hand, were everything Lizzie tried to avoid with all her energy, because she had chosen freedom instead.

"No, I got some. But a Stella would be great."

Arrogant kings of the inside.

Where Lizzie didn't want to be, having decided differently when her parents had told her that she could do whatever she wanted to do.

That she could become whatever she wanted to become.

That it was her own choice.

"Would have brought you one anyway," Amanda said.

Then.

When, between the lamb roast and the strawberry dessert, absolute freedom had been declared. When, sitting around the family dining table, they had all nodded.

And smiled.

And agreed, because there had simply been nothing to disagree with; to rebel against your parents at the family dining table would have meant to do the exact opposite of what you wanted to do.

Naturally, no one did that.

Naturally, everyone went out to become whatever they wanted to become and so Lizzie went out to become an artist and now it would be Claire wanting to know if it could still be done. Once again, it would be Claire wondering if the dream was still alive; would Lizzie still be able to say yes?

"I'll give you cash afterwards."

But Amanda was already out of the door and onto the streets of London.

Paved with opportunity.

Paved with a promise.

Then.

When, talking life and talking the future, everyone had genuinely believed what everyone had been saying, constantly:

That everything was possible.

Jonathan dropped the plastic fork into the brown box in front of him, where the neglected pita bread soaked the remaining garlic sauce; had he really passed out on Kingsland Road this morning?

He pushed the box away.

To be discarded, a job done and on, towards the stuff that really counted:

The night's first bar; a brand new straw.

It had only taken a moment or so to discard the unorthodox idea that had carefully knocked, as he had woken from three hours of semi-drunk afternoon sleep:

Not to go out, for a change?

A joke.

It had only taken a moment or so to know that he had to go on immediately, as last night's picture had finally stopped being fuzzy: the gate, a man, a fiver. Cans of Red Stripe sold from a makeshift bar and then a drawer, underneath, but not selling alcohol.

"Heavy night?"

The stakes had been raised again.

That much was clear.

"Tell me about it, man," Jonathan said, because there was no need for lies in front of those meat skewers:

"Lost my mobile too."

"What again?"

"Yes."

Adem, Hakan and Mustafa were the only people in this world who knew it all: the sex, the drugs, the chicken shish. The lost mobile phones and the lost belief in everything that didn't take place at night and here.

Had he really been robbed by a bunch of Hackney bastards as he had lain unconscious and helpless on a Friday morning Kingsland Road?

The lost plot in the eyes of all those that had no idea what kind of plots this particular life was writing.

"Here, have a Stella," Mustafa said, and:

"Look like you need it."

"I do man, cheers," Jonathan said, because, in here, there was no need for the pre-watershed take for all those that didn't understand the life Jonathan liked to live, seeking nothing but pleasure and finding it on every corner of his city.

In here, there was no need to edit out the bloodshed.

Jonathan opened the can.

Adem, Hakan and Mustafa eased him enough to let his defences rest a little. Sitting on his wobbly small table, while supposedly funny Turkish chat shows flickered over the small TV set on the wall of what had become his living room, he could almost be himself.

"Can I have cigarettes as well, please?" he half-whispered, since they came from Poland, and sometimes Russia, and from underneath the counter, sparing Jonathan the dreaded 4am alone and without.

"Red ones?" Mustafa said and Jonathan nodded; always the red ones, never the Lights, full of five hundred chemicals, tasting of nothing.

Always forward, never back.

Always higher, looking for cracks in the now, because in the past there weren't any:

A happy parade.

A carefree ride.

A paradise Jonathan had left behind, because families and friends were only obstacles on his way to real satisfaction, the good life replaced by class A, casual sex and yet another pint of whatever.

Jonathan ripped away the plastic.

That was what the city did to you. But Jonathan had stopped blaming the city.

He took out a fag and got up.

"Cheers, guys."

Out there, they would already be streaming, from buses to bars.

"See you soon."

Out there, they would already be moving as most humans preferred to move, in herds, and that meant that Jonathan had to hurry up.

"Yep."

At the counter, he passed the black-haired girl from next door's pole-and-mirror Axe, who knew about the cigarettes too, and two firm buttocks in tight, shiny leggings were enough to wake exactly what needed waking, just as yesterday's substances started their day-after dance.

All of a sudden, there was no doubt about this at all anymore:

The stray dog was ready to stray again.

Jonathan had another sip.

In his veins, a slow-burning sensation met his desperate need for a cigarette and started turning, sip by sip by sip, into the insatiable hunger that caught him night after night, just at the moment Jonathan heard:

"Do you think my friend's attractive?"

She twisted her blonde curls underneath a black trilby hat; was it that late already, would-be drunks starting to talk to strangers on Hackney Road, because their group behaviour was boring the living shit out of them?

"Course she is," Jonathan said and lit up and dragged. Creating the base for this body to function.

"You see, I told you," she said.

Jonathan smiled.

The blonde-haired girl's friend wasn't attractive at all; the blonde-haired girl was very attractive indeed.

"So what are you up to?"

What did it look like?

"Was out with some friends, but they just left," he said, hiding the stray dog to impress, and:

"I was hoping to bump into two pretty girls and convince them for a last drink."

"You're living in London?" the unattractive one said, not getting anything at all.

"Of course he is," the attractive one said, finally picking up on the look Jonathan was giving her, confident eyes married to a friendly smile, the most powerful weapon he had. This would be a good night.

All the signs were there.

"You like it?"

He loved it, adored it and needed it more than anything: the sirens and the dirt. The holes in the street. The smell that changed on every corner.

Jonathan nodded.

He was addicted to the noise of a tube, screeching to a halt, and the sound of a black cab, speeding away. He lived on the orange shine that covered these streets at night.

"So, you're up for a drink?"

This was both the best and the worst place to live, where you could get anything you wanted. Except quality of life.

And who needed that?

"Jane, our bus!"

"Hold on..." Jonathan said, but the unattractive one said:

"We can't miss this one!"

She pulled her friend out of Jonathan's reach.

Why were people even bothering going out if they wanted to be back for the 10 o' clock news?

"Nice chatting," the attractive one said, as she was being pushed towards a 48 picking up early leavers, still twisting her curls in front of a daring cleavage.

Goodbye and thanks for spoiling the party before it had even started.

Jonathan had a deep drag.

Goodbye and thanks for crushing expectations that were high enough now for Jonathan to know that there was only one possible outcome. That, having been tickled like that, there was only one natural conclusion, potential victims in every bar and execution in experienced hands, and that was:

Full-on attack.

Max teetered forward and back on his swivel chair; it took half an hour to cook dinner and it took two weeks to read a good book. It took three years to get a degree and a lifetime to make sense of this world. How long did it take to be certain that someone you didn't know understood you better than anyone else ever had?

Max still couldn't believe it.

He adjusted his headset.

There wasn't nearly enough light in this small room off Shoreditch High Street, and there was almost no air, but there was nothing anyone could do about it:

A cubicle.

A job.

A life.

Max still couldn't get his head around the electrifying words heard and spoken a few hours earlier, over in the canteen area, when an "Unknown Caller" had turned into a journalist, but if he wanted to keep this job, he needed to get another interview now.

He hit the dial key.

The massive clock on the wall opposite was crawling towards this evening shift's end, but, in here, every hour lasted a day; Max stared at his monochrome screen.

In here, Max had no other option, but to trick another innocent pensioner into answering questions she couldn't even hear, switching on his headset and switching off his brain, staring ahead...

Because for out there, he had higher plans.

He twisted the black cord; a conversation that didn't want to let go wanted to come on again, but in front of him his mobile started announcing a call from someone who still didn't understand a thing:

"How's the job hunt going, son?"

Max looked left and right again, but the two supervisors seemed to be patrolling another row of this prison. He pressed the cancel button on his sticky keyboard and leaned back in his chair.

"Mum, it's not a good time to talk."

"I just thought, I hear again..."

"What do you expect me to say, Mum? Honestly. It's not that easy, you see?"

It was a bloody battle.

"Yes, well..."

And no one could accuse him of not fighting this battle with all his energy, twisting and turning a life he could, by now, cite like a poem: the right word, inserted at the right place. The polished phrases, put as expected. The dumb little lies that made up a life, spun for maximum impression, re-arranged, copy-and-paste, to be used, cap in hand, for another bow.

For another cry.

For another plea to those deciding over life and death, for a chance to be allowed inside.

"So, no news then?"

Ending this battle once and for all.

"Mum, do you really think I wouldn't call you straight away if there were any news?"

After all those attempts, two years and counting, trying to stay alive in a world that required people to lie into headsets in order to survive, in order to be able to, eventually, make their contribution to make this world a better place.

"Yes, I suppose..."

After all those emails introducing their second paragraph with the word "unfortunately".

"Okay then," she said, because, apparently, there wasn't anything else to talk about anymore now.

"Right."

Apparently, the battle had erased the being outstanding at school and the shining at university and had killed all the pride of past achievements which now, one failed application after another, paled into insignificance. Forgotten efforts in vain that only left Max unable to find a job.

Max, the dreamer.

Max, the loser.

"Dad was wondering if you hadn't tried something different."

Max, the idiot.

"Mum."

And all that hadn't been the deal. People like him, with degrees like him and grades like him and motivation like him weren't meant to hear all this, over and over again.

"Well, Max..."

"Look Mum, I have to go."

People like him, with ambitions like him and ideas like him and dreams like him weren't meant to say, again and again, okay and amen and sorry.

"Okay, son."

And no one had understood that better than someone called Sarah.

Max adjusted his headset again.

He pulled himself closer to the table in front of him and hit the dial key; how patiently she had listened to every word Max had uttered, painful details pouring out in an openness he hadn't even known existed.

About one failed attempt after the next.

About despair, taking over?

About evening after evening spent staring at the same black sans-serif on a white background, getting up and sitting down and getting up again.

About the battle in all its frustrating and soul-destroying guises, following him wherever Max went.

"Go on..."

About the slogan that was shining in big neon letters, when waking up and when making coffee and when cycling to the call centre and when cycling back and when lying in bed trying desperately to fall asleep:

Not to give up.

Not to surrender quite yet, because battle-hardened fighters like him would rest instead, and recover, and attack just the way they had before.

As if they had never tried before.

Max looked at his mobile.

As if they had never lost before.

Because Max wasn't prepared to work for years and years in a job he didn't like and wasn't good at only to, eventually, be rewarded. Only to, eventually, be allowed to do what Max wanted to do right away and she had understood this so perfectly, hadn't she?

That Max wanted to make a difference and wasn't prepared to settle for less.

He had to get in touch again.

There was no question.

He looked at the newspaper that was still lying next to him, neatly folded. Delivering, column for column, reasons to act. Dishing up, page for page, other people's opinions, while his lines remained unheard.

He could text her straight away.

She had given him her mobile number at the end of the interview.

Max took off his headset and grabbed his phone; she had said, with a little laugh Max hadn't been able to read:

"Just in case, you know."

Sarah carried a glass of wine from the kitchen to the living room and slumped onto the Chesterfield couch, where she looked at herself in the large mirror that didn't really fit their flat's decoration, but was too pretty to throw away, awkwardly hanging next to the painting Peter had bought to celebrate his last promotion:

"So," she said to herself, and:

"How was your day?"

That was the ritual, settling into a comfort zone guarded by the soldiers in position.

Fifty eight square metres of calm amid London's noise.

Sarah had a sip.

Fifty eight square metres of sanity amid the madness.

And another.

Fifty eight square metres of certainty in an uncertain world and one glass of wine to relax a tension that had become an undercurrent: always there, but not acute enough to worry Sarah.

"Alright," she answered.

A to-do list, worked through. A duty, performed. A professional salary earned, which, even subtracting the mortgage payments, allowed them the comfortable lifestyle Sarah had grown used to.

"Alright?"

She started smiling.

"Just that?"

She took up the mobile phone that was lying in front of her; Peter would be here any minute now.

Should she really do this?

She pressed the reply-button, but Peter's keys started rattling the same moment, the front door swinging open to the sound of his excited sing-sang:

"Hey, are you ready for the news?"

She placed the mobile back on the table.

"Sure. If you sit down first."

"Yes, sorry."

Peter slumped down next to Sarah, who was expecting a modest promotion, and said without preparation:

"They're sending me to Berlin."

Another small step on the ladder.

"What?"

"Fantastic, isn't it?"

Peter placed his right hand on her left leg, but the synthetic fabric of her long pinstripe skirt didn't allow affection, only a numb sense of touch, work wear like a uniform.

"It's a new project and they want me to be in charge, isn't that wonderful, Sarah?"

She turned towards the triumphant sparkle of victory that had taken over his eyes and nodded. The game, finally, turning his way. His manoeuvres, paying off. The strategy, chewed over and over again with her, delivering a result.

"It is, Peter," she said and turned away again.

"It really is."

Reacting like a professional women was expected to react to news like that. All hail to the future.

All hail to getting on.

"Three months. Possibly even longer," he said, and:

"Hey, but I'll just have a quick shower and then we'll celebrate properly, okay?"

Sarah nodded.

Three months and possibly longer without being asked about her day and without being kissed goodnight – that would be a whole new situation for a relationship that had long become the real deal, sharing problems, a bed, life. Buying vegetables from Fresh & Wild after work and sex once a week, usually.

"Who were you writing?", Peter said and got up.

"What?"

"Who were you writing?"

"Oh, no one."

She had a quick sip.

"But you have a new message open here."

"Really?" she said and leaned forward.

"Must have happened accidentally."

"They're sending me to Berlin, Sarah, can you believe it? It's going to be so exciting. And three months will be okay for us, don't you think?"

Sarah nodded.

All hail to getting on, climbing up, taking over.

"It's amazing, Peter. It really is."

Peter turned around, leaving Sarah staring into the mirror without seeing anything, her vision blurred from too much input:

Her comfort zone was on fire.

The soldiers were confused:

"Dear Sarah, there are some important details I forgot to mention when we talked earlier and I think they would really enhance your article. I would appreciate if we could talk again," and:

"Perhaps in person this time?"

It would look totally silly to reply to this, but wasn't that exactly what intrigued her?

She crossed her legs, from right to left.

Wasn't that the price she had to pay if she wanted to find out what had happened to her as she had listened, her pen abandoned, to passions she had forgotten existed, because they had faded away a long time ago?

"See you in a bit," Peter said.

"Yes, okay."

Sarah picked up the mobile again.

Wasn't that the daring step she had to take if she wanted to get another chance to hear the beliefs, undistorted?

The words Sarah had known herself, once.

The kind of unrealistic ambition that only existed on the other side of a sweet surrender that, five years in, Sarah had accepted with a shrug, living her life inside a box that was warm and safe and cosy and protected by a trigger-happy squad that had looked nervous the moment Sarah had started to leave the script behind:

"Well, it's not really the idea of an interview for the journalist to be asked questions, but go ahead."

She put down the mobile again.

It had all just poured out, entering the tube with her student pass showing a girl smiling as naïve and innocent as a young girl smiled on a student tube pass. So inexperienced. So clueless. Entering an office, as everyone was having gap years and lazy summers.

"Wow."

"Well."

It had all just come out like never before, picking up the phone for the first time, sounding proud and confident. Dressing smartly and taking mobile calls on buses. Staying in the office until midnight to savour a feeling that had started the moment she had touched her staff ID on the reader for the first time.

As if to say welcome.

As if to say that she was one of them now and a grateful smile had taken over her face as it had sunk in properly that she had arrived, was on board, finally, in charge and important and had been kicking off like no one else.

"Wow."

"Well."

There was no other option, was there?

She had to reply.

It would look totally unprofessional, but there was no other way to tell her full story, five years in.

She crossed her legs, from left to right.

She picked up the mobile again.

She crossed her legs, from right to left; what was there to lose?

Oh Catch, Shoreditch.

Tight skirts were rubbing against the skinny jeans as red lips sucked their relief through chewed-on straws.

Oh Catch, Shoreditch.

Around Lizzie, pints of Grolsch were being ordered, shots of Sambuca downed.

She pushed her way through the crowd.

Around Lizzie, fellow desperates waved twenty pound notes in a vain attempt to get seen, served, satisfied from behind the comforting row of silver taps, promising, as they always did, escape.

Promising, as they always did, the world.

Lizzie had a deep breath.

Oh Catch, Shoreditch.

Ready to deliver exactly what Lizzie needed after Claire and half a bottle of wine. Throwing it right into her face, the sweet perfume of sweat and sex that conveniently covered worries unneeded for this jump into another East London night; Lizzie had a sip from her Whisky Coke.

Oh last hope.

This was her rescue after two hours of looking for progress and looking for success and looking for words and not finding any of it. She had admitted her slow surrender; she had conceded that time was running out.

She had survived two hours of whine and counter whine.

She wasn't prepared to give up.

Lizzie squeezed past a group of girls standing at the edge of the small dance floor and fell right against eyes that were sparkling in a kind of blue that was impossible to ignore.

"Hi there," he said.

Right against eyes that were grabbing her by the throat.

"Do I know you?" she said.

"Not yet."

"Okay…" she said and took a step back and he took a step forward and she said:

"So, you're here alone?"

"Yeah. Well, all my friends have gone, but I'm not willing to go anywhere without music, lights and a bar."

"Tell me about it."

"So you're alone, too?" he said.

"Well, yeah, I…just a last drink, you know?"

To which he smiled the kind of smile that seemed to say that words weren't needed, because he knew exactly what Lizzie was talking about, last-drink-alone accusations left to those that had no idea what this kind of life was about.

"Hey, do you think I could be an actress?"

It just burst out.

This was the question that had been burning inside of her ever since she had left the pub and Lizzie fired it without even a second thought.

"An actress? Hell, yeah. Aren't you one already?"

She wanted this lingering doubt, taken.

"No I'm not, I'm an artist."

"No big difference, is it?"

"Yeah well, that's the point, kind of."

"What's the point?"

"A friend just asked me why I didn't try acting, for a change. Because the other stuff isn't quite, you know, working out."

Even though Claire wasn't the person to suggest a thing like this, having tried nothing at all since leaving university.

"You definitely should," he said.

It was a channel of sorts, wasn't it?

And it was a channel Lizzie hadn't considered yet. She had grabbed whatever one could grab on her ride towards becoming not just good, but great, having swapped pens for a paintbrush. Having dropped shutters to pick up a spatula.

She had tried every possible option.

But acting?

Her road was littered with failures and she was running out of ideas, but here was a new option.

"You really think so?"

Here was a new chance.

"Absolutely. Look at you, you have the looks of an actress. You have... I mean, your eyes..."

He just looked into them.

What was going on here, cheesy compliments overruling the die-hard decision that Lizzie had enough problems without boys entering the equation?

"So do you come here often?" she said, quickly.

He nodded.

What was it about this stranger that made her want to keep talking?

"It used to be my living room," he said and moved a little closer. Crossing the line between chat-up and conversation. Making the point that this was between her and him now.

"So what's the actress's name?"

Lizzie laughed.

"Hey, I haven't even decided to actually go for it, so... Do you really think it's a good idea? I'm Lizzie, by the way," and:

"So who are you?"

But before he could answer, the speakers died, all of a sudden, and sent a massive roar from one side of the room to the other, causing all the drunken souls to fear for the worst, a dance floor riot in the making:

Desperates of all convictions unite.

Causing Lizzie to look into the stranger's eyes again.

Deeper.

And deeper until the sound returned and the DJ kicked off, as if to say sorry, with Blue Monday, which meant that he started moving, as if by slight-of-hand, and meant that Lizzie started moving too, and meant that, before she knew any better, she was dancing with him, close and far and closer and hearing right into her left ear:

"I really like you, Lizzie."

Ha!

Without knowing her at all, a mean lie uttered without care, but Lizzie's usual urge to object was disabled by a smile that was half come-and-chat friendly and half come-and-fuck sexy and a hundred percent drunk at the same time, which was a confusing mix, but not distracting from the fact that he was a good dancer, with legs that were moving, it seemed, without asking him, until the song blended into the next.

"Hey, how about another drink?"

Lizzie nodded.

"Whisky Coke, please."

Assurance in a glass, please. Cold and solid. Something to cling to, please.

"Another thing we have in common," he said, still standing much closer to her than any stranger should after such a short time. After so few words.

Should she really have a go at acting?

Was that really her last chance to avoid the same scenes at Christmas, all eyes on her and nothing to say?

"I'll get us two," he said, but before he could turn around the DJ made true her threat and choked her sounds without even so much as a warning, brushing away panicky pleas from all those that were only half way there, and Lizzie was looking into a face that was saying, without uttering a single word:

"Let's not go home."

And Lizzie replied, without opening her mouth:

"Not quite yet."

And he grabbed her hand and led her through the sorry line-up of tip-toeing amateurs, clumsily clinging because they didn't have a plan B, and through the narrow door, onto Kingsland Road, where mini cabs were grating glass splinters into the gutter and the winter wind smacked their glowing faces with a reassuring mix of cigarette smoke and cheap kebab meat.

"Can I have one too?" Lizzie said.

"Sure."

He lit both cigarettes and started inhaling and exhaling as if his life depended on it.

"And I still don't know your name," Lizzie said.

Despite being grabbed like that.

She looked at him.

Despite being taken away past Red Planet Pizza and past Jaguar Shoes and, without any resistance, beneath the disused old railway bridge, where the siren of an ambulance echoed away all other sounds.

"Russian Bar?" he said.

"Russian Bar," she said and felt his right arm coming up around her waist.

Max pedalled on.

The cold air of night wrapped his face. He evaded the street's massive potholes as he entered Kingsland Road's darkest stretch, where crumbling warehouses, council rows and swanky new developments sat next to each other as if they were shadows. This day was supposed to be over. The clock was somewhere between one and two. He was supposed to be tired, but, unfortunately, he wasn't.

Unfortunately, he couldn't stop.

He was meant to calm down, but instead he pedalled faster, up the road and further into deepest, darkest Hackney, which had long become another brightly-lit, carefree playground for the likes of him, overeducated and spoilt.

But there was hardly any input at all on this stretch, which meant that this mind had no other choice but to grab another tried and tested spark in its attempt to push away a conversation that refused to leave:

Everyone wanted to belong to a generation.

No one wanted to belong to this generation.

Because this generation, for the first time ever, didn't deserve the term.

Because this generation, for the first time ever, was bound together by nothing, but Ikea shelves:

Billy, but no idea.

Max shook his head; on the right, the neon-signs of the all-night shop and the mini cab office and the fish restaurant announced new life. On his left, the Lockner Estate stretched behind its brick wall as if it was never to end. The Haggerston was spilling its pint-clutching parade of drunkenness onto the pavement and the small side street that was leading east.

But Max kept going straight.

He pedalled like an idiot, because the distraction he had tried since leaving the call centre, reading the comment pages of yet another newspaper over Vietnamese food at Song Que, followed by three slow-motion pints in a bar he had never been to, had done nothing to take this away:

"So what exactly do you want to become Max?"

"Whatever it takes."

Because everything had to change if this world wanted a chance and no one knew that better than Max. Something radical had to happen, but he hadn't been nearly as specific as he should have been in response to that question and his only chance to correct that was the meeting he had proposed by text, and now, all he could do was to do what he was doing anyway.

And that was to wait.

Now, all he could do was to stick to the habit of a generation that, for the first time ever, was simply that:

An age bracket.

United in nothing, but this simmering sense of despair, because it knew better than any other generation that this was everyone:

Alone.

Max jerked his handlebars to the right.

"Moron," he heard.

It should have been him, shouting the same word at this stumbling drunk, but justice had long left the streets of London, and this stumbling drunk knew that as much as Max did.

"Moron, eh?"

Max turned left again; a stumbling drunk wasn't nearly enough to distract a mind that was still fighting a conversation that kept bubbling with a truth that had been troubling Max for some time now:

Everyone wanted to claim a decade.

No one wanted to claim this decade.

Because this was the decade during which everything had collapsed.

First, the towers.

Then, the banks.

Then: hope?

And no one wanted to be associated with collapse. No one wanted to claim the loss of hope.

Max shook his head; this had been nine eleven and seven seven and nothing in between and now, it was nearly over. Now, it was nearly gone, and, unfortunately, it had passed much quicker than anyone would have thought that chilly night, when the computers hadn't crashed, after all, but, drunken and delirious, everyone had been cheering loudly:

To the millennium!

To greater things!

To their decade, which had so kindly asked them to be shaped, and to everyone doing all the things that, looking back, they hadn't done, after all, leaving them right here, right now, grabbing whatever they could grab:

Hadn't his text sounded totally silly? Was that the reason she wasn't replying?

Max ignored what was left and what was right.

Max pedalled on.

This was him, trapped inside a head where warmed-up beliefs were once again hunting half-cooked slogans that would never see the light of day.

This was him, going on.

An alien, of sorts, when he had arrived here and an alien, of sorts, still, cycling through another night surrounded by seven million aliens that were glued together by six letters.

And not much else.

Max flew into a green-light junction and into Dalston Lane, where the majestic white cranes announced a development no one around here wanted to see developed, a whole stretch reduced to ruins in the name of a so-called future, when the real future had to look so very different.

Max sighed.

The future...

But who was listening to him?

The torturous question had started imposing itself again and there was nothing he could do:

Who gave a toss what he had to say about a future world that had abolished an economy that was still swallowing up everything this planet was running out of, and quickly, because it was still based on nothing but growth?

As if growth was unlimited.

As if everything was.

Who cared what he had to say about a future world, where borders had ceased to exist and countries had ceased to matter and a real rethink had started to hail the 21st Century, once and for all?

Max stopped at the red light.

He had so much to give, but no one gave a shit, least of all those shielded from the world's bad news by a garden fence. Having arrived where they had arrived via the given path, because for them there had only been the one:

What idea did they have?

Sitting in their armchairs of experience, his parents were expecting what parents could expect, not understanding for a minute what was really going on.

Here, on the outside.

Where it was getting colder by the day.

Max stared at the red light.

All these were good thoughts; these thoughts had to be written down, thought further. As so often, these thoughts were screaming to be refined, worked on, sharpened. If only he had a way to release them.

If only he had a way...

These thoughts were asking to be used, published, heard, but if he didn't take care, he would lose them somewhere between chaining his bike and scanning the newly delivered magazines, brimming with thoughts other people had written down, thought further, refined, worked on and sharpened. Full of the brilliance other people had published because other people had jobs that allowed them to publish things.

And make a difference.

Unlike Max, who was wearing a headset instead and repeated the same meaningless questions to innocent pensioners, just because he was clinging to a vague notion that eventually he, too, would arrive where this journalist had arrived a long time ago.

In his pocket, the mobile vibrated.

He started smiling.

The light switched from red to green; that was it, wasn't it? That would be the text message that would allow him to calm down, finally, and close his eyes and fall asleep, safe in the knowledge that he would get one more chance to explain himself properly.

"So?" Sarah said.

In their window, the apron-clad pancake ladies were kneading their dough bathed in a mellow morning light. Café Evin, the Turkish café on Kingsland High Street he had suggested in a very excited reply to her careful Friday night text, was early Monday busy.

"Ahm..."

Breakfast eaters were sitting next to young mums chatting about their sleepless night, while here and there, a member of the freelancing brigade had plugged in a laptop, chatting away on a mobile, asking this, claiming that. On this window table, there was an eerie silence.

"Yes?"

He was still looking as nervous as you would for a job interview, awkwardly clenching the cup in front of him, still filled to the top with coffee that had to be cold by now.

"Well, I don't know. It was just that..."

He looked into his cup.

"It's just that..."

"Just what?"

Sarah looked at her watch; she was already 15 minutes late for work, but there was nothing she could do. She had told Max that this breakfast meeting at the bottom of Stoke Newington High Street was business.

That this was work, after all.

When it was anything but.

She had told him that it would be no problem at all, meeting him here before going to the office, Café Evin being on the way, but now, half an hour into this encounter, she had to leave and couldn't, hearing Max mumble, finally:

"I just thought that I came across as someone who had no idea what to do with his life, you know."

Sarah nodded.

"Well, yes, you did, kind of."

He stared at her.

"But you also came across as someone who had a hundred ideas on a hundred other things," she said.

Here she was.

Peter had left for Berlin this morning; the rushed timing of his new life had only been revealed with the second glass of wine on Friday night, but now it was a reality already, one of her fixed points in life: gone.

She leaned forward a little.

She said:

"You know, if you ask people what they want to do with their lives, they usually tell you what they want to become: journalists, architects, whatever. A profession, a life."

Max started smiling a little.

"A job, a purpose, if you like. Filling all the space available. But if you ask these people what they actually want to do as journalists or architects or whatever, they don't know what to say. If you ask them what they actually want to do with their lives, they run out of words. Don't you think?"

She glanced out of the window for a second, than back at Max. The fire in his eyes was only partly concealing his nervousness. The expression on his face was begging her to go on.

"And as far as I recall, that's when you started," she said.

Was this really Sarah speaking?

Explaining the world as she never had, not even to herself. Why was she feeling so at ease next to this stranger?

Max just nodded.

"So, don't you worry," she said and checked her watch again, showing her restlessness with increasing obviousness.

But Max just said:

"So tell me about writing. It must be absolutely amazing to be able to do this for a living."

Explaining the world, but not hers.

"Well," Sarah said.

She shuffled around a little on her chair, eyes to the street, then back to him, then to the street again.

Not explaining the touching in. And not explaining the touching out, either.

Not explaining the in-between, whatever the in-between was, five years in.

Not explaining that it was shocking not to know what the in-between was, five years in.

"It's okay," Sarah said.

Shocking to have long lost what someone else still had, eyes glowing with excitement. Shocking to have lost what seemed so terribly important, once.

"Just okay?" Max said, but Sarah looked down a little. She couldn't tell about the jumping in.

About the growing comfortable.

About learning the rules and about playing by them, quicker than you would have imagined in your wildest dreams.

She couldn't tell about saying the right things to the right people and about keeping quiet about other things.

About adjusting your needs to that of your employer and putting their beliefs before yours.

She couldn't say a word about the soldiers.

"Anyway, thanks so much," Max said, finally sensing her growing unease, or her shuffling around, or both.

"What for?"

"Well, for, you know, meeting me. I guess it's not something you usually do?"

She looked at him.

Was her meticulously constructed façade of officialdom already crashing down in front of her?

"Well," she said.

Had the stranger already sensed that this Turkish pancake breakfast wasn't about the piece for the magazine or a stupid detail he had forgotten to convey over the phone?

"Well," she said again.

Had Max already understood that this wasn't really about him at all?

"Sometimes we do," she said.

She picked up her phone from the table in front of her and pretended to read a message that had never arrived.

"Listen, Max, I have to run. There's someone I need to see in the office in half an hour."

She got up.

"It was a pleasure talking to you."

"Okay, no problem," Max said and got up too.

"And likewise..."

Sarah got into her winter coat and took her bag from underneath their table, consciously over-playing the role of a professional woman in a sudden hurry, having received orders that had to be obeyed, life's reality on full show.

She stretched out her hand.

"Thanks again," Max said, shaking it.

"All the best for you."

Sarah turned around, pushed the door and stepped outside without looking back. On the other side of the street, a 149 was ready to return her to the given track, down the street and further inside, so she could touch in, slump down and play her part.

Sarah crossed the street.

So the soldiers could have their deep breath of relief, a full hour overdue; if only it wasn't impossible to push away what had happened the moment they had started talking properly in there.

Lizzie braved the onslaught.

A hundred languages were hitting her thought-wrapped face as she turned onto Kingsland High Street. A hundred different sounds were fighting a hundred different smells as if that was the most natural thing on earth and Lizzie stepped left to evade a trolley-pushing old lady, and right to give way to a jumpy madman in zigzag, and left again, avoiding a girl that was running from her mother, shouting, shouting, shouting.

Lizzie jumped.

This was her Kingsland walk and, usually, she managed it to perfection, but on this particular Monday morning, she only just about managed to avoid crashing into a power-driven wheelchair breaking all speed limits.

Jesus!

On this particular Monday morning, Lizzie was really still standing at the dingy counter of a Friday night Russian Bar, where she had heard:

"Come on, Lizzie. One last Whisky Coke."

Lizzie could still feel his soft hands around her waist as he had half-whispered into her right ear:

"You can't refuse this, queen of the stage."

There was something dangerous about this man.

There was something she couldn't point at.

"Can't I?"

The Russian was two days ago now, another weekend without movement endured, but the scene didn't leave, dancing close, and far, and closer; Lizzie stopped to let through an out-of-breath crawler carrying more orange shopping bags than anyone should carry along a walkway in a constant state of jam, only to see her getting passed by two over-confident amateurs, promptly running into a grinning drunk drifter, who started hurling terms of abuse he was surely making up as he went along.

Lizzie let her fingers glide through her hair:

This haircut worked.

She was all set.

"Why don't we try something a little more conservative?" she had told Mario half an hour ago.

Because life was like that:

You chose.

"Con-ser-vative?"

Lizzie had managed to get the morning's first appointment without even calling, but there had to be some advantage to working in a hair salon. It didn't make good the damage the shampoo caused to her hands and it didn't cancel out the boredom she felt in there pretty much all the time, but having the most senior stylist at her disposal for a constantly changing wish list of experiments was at least something.

Because, if nothing else changed, the hairstyle had to.

"Is there a particular reason, if you don't mind me asking?" Mario had said, half an hour ago, and Lizzie had mumbled something about just a feeling, when this was so much more than that:

Here was a brand new chance.

Here was another option, as suggested by Claire, sitting on a dimly lit table of The Royal Oak, Columbia Road.

Here was a crazy idea that, after God knew how many Whisky Cokes, hadn't seemed that crazy anymore. Doubt for doubt had been pushed away by another dance in between those large mirrors that made the Russian Bar look like a strip club. Worry for worry had been taken by a complete stranger.

The plan to become an actress:

Made?

Everything was about to change forever, but Mario couldn't have sensed any of it. Pulling here and pulling there, Mario must have thought that the glow in Lizzie's eyes had been about a clear fringe and a brown tone. He couldn't have sensed that, for a change, Lizzie's anticipation wasn't about her new hairstyle at all:

She could do this, couldn't she?

She had pulled a few strings already: Her friend Frieda was on the case.

Lizzie smiled.

Because here was a new chance, waiting to be grabbed with both hands.

And Lizzie was ready.

Dangling in front of her eyes, was an opportunity that would not just make Lizzie good, but great, rescuing her in the very last minute from all eyes on her, sinking down further and further on a kitchen table where, once, absolute freedom had been declared, but, now, progress was expected.

This was the one.

Lizzie passed the shopping centre and turned right, where the smell of fish announced her home. She started pushing her way through the crowds that filled the walkway between Ridley Road's market stalls without much breathing space. She got squeezed:

This was a terrible mistake!

She pushed back.

Wouldn't this only end in failure, just like last month's clumsy try, putting another half-dream into reality? Putting papier-mâché onto a metal structure only to watch the whole thing collapse into a miserable pile of material mess, leaving Lizzie, once again:

Refusing a fight.

Leaving Lizzie, once again, with no other option, but to run, more damage done.

Lizzie needed a nod!

Lizzie needed another word of support from someone who had been on her side straight away, leaving her uncertainties outside a sticky East London bar to run, one more time, into the arms of someone who understood:

"You're right."

"I know."

She turned left.

The smell that entered her nostrils changed from fish to meat to sweat to frankincense. She stepped over a slippery layer of rotten tomatoes and cardboard mush to reach her rackety front door, but she didn't enter the flat.

She took a deep breath.

She could blame God, naturally.

She could point at his way of passing a dull Friday night, sitting on a fluffy white cloud, or wherever it was he was sitting, playing board games, of sorts, with every other city another board and with London, the premium edition, where he had all the figures at once.

Where the possibilities were endless.

But Lizzie didn't believe in God and, in any case, God was far too easy an explanation.

A convenient way out of too many situations.

A lazy answer to too many questions and, by now, most people got that.

If Lizzie believed in God, she would blame him, having picked two figures at random, just to place them on the fringe of a sweaty Shoreditch dance floor.

Just to see what would happen.

She took out her mobile and leaned against the wall.

But this was real life.

"Hi there," she wrote.

This was what happened: people collided. In the streets and in the bars. On tubes and on night buses.

"Lizzie here."

This was the city, where lives constantly touched, but usually without effect.

Usually without consequences.

"From Friday night."

And then, sometimes, they did in a way no one quite understood, not even God, sitting up there on his fluffy white cloud, or wherever he was sitting.

And then, anything could happen.

Zigzag lines turned into weird circles and the corners became the centre on a flicker screen that seemed to constantly change colour, even though it wasn't, and breathing out again, Jonathan tried hard not to vomit all over a keyboard that was sneering a little more with every minute it remained untouched:

Another night.

Another story.

"You alright, Johnnybuddy?" Mark shouted from his desk opposite; another name Jonathan would forget.

What did it look like?

"You've been drinking, eh? Honestly, mate, on a Sunday night?"

Mark shook his head.

"Bad boy."

What difference did it make, every night as suitable as the next for a stray dog to have three cans and a line, storming out as if it had been the first time ever, down the forsaken side streets and along Hackney Road, for another straw.

"Whatever," Jonathan said.

Another episode that would fade away as soon as the next one would come along, drinking other people's vodka from plastic cups in a flat on Pitfield Street, having embraced this city's randomness, once again to hear:

"You crashed the party, eh?"

Having simply walked in.

To see this cute grin:

"Well, just so you know, it's my party and I'm Kate and I think you're sweet and we should have another drink."

And then, and not much later, things had worked out as they were supposed to, blonde curls tickling his naked chest.

"Need painkillers, mate?"

Mark looked at him, but Jonathan shook his head, slowly; he had Aspirin three hundred and he had Paracetamol five hundred, but he had longed for at least two thousand this morning, as he had nicked a few cigarettes from the table in the living room, where the lifeless bodies had scattered.

Another connection, cut.

Why had he been unable to do the same on Friday night? A perfectly suitable victim, a perfectly suitable night.

For this?

The five year old mobile phone he was forced to use now was still lying in front of him, displaying a message that needed more thinking than he was able to muster this morning, or any morning.

Jonathan pushed it a little, left, right, left, right:

There was no way he would reply to this.

He had already violated the most important rule. Standing in the dawn outside the Russian Bar, where the minicab driver had battled it out for their custom, the girl that had refused to play by the rules all night had simply slipped away, holding something he should never have handed out:

A name.

A number.

A trace.

"Thanks for a great night, mysterious stranger," she had said and had vanished. Standing in the dawn outside the Russian Bar, his defences had failed him for one crucial moment and that had handed him the fatal consequences now lying on the table in front of him, left, right, left.

Jonathan pushed the mobile away.

There was no way he would grant her that follow-up and there was no way in the world he would grant her that follow-up in a Dalston pub as tame as The George on a Monday, where only couples and small groups would occupy the tables, smacking their togetherness into everyone's face.

Leaving no way for the stray dog to attack.

"You smell terrible, by the way."

"Shut up, Mark," Jonathan said, and:

"Just shut up."

"How's the project coming along then?"

Jonathan didn't answer.

It was the only way, that much was clear, surviving life, one project at the time, in this musty office, just like out there, tick and move. Click and go. Cut and run, from one project to the next, no ballast or overhang or anything:

Looking back was forbidden.

"Do we still have coffee?"

"Nope. You're drinking too much of it anyway, don't you think? I mean, I'm not your mother, but..."

But life was a perfect circle, which meant drinking coffee all day to cure the hangover only to leave the office so dehydrated that the only cure was a pint.

Followed by another.

"Damn it," Jonathan said, slowly pulling up his defences to keep the unsettling truths of his existence away from those that didn't understand.

He pushed away the mobile.

Moving on with a shrug. As intended, feeling responsible for no one, but himself.

"By the way Johnnybuddy, I have this invitation for a press thing tonight. At The Light, I think, this Shoreditch place. Free drinks and the lot. The national press is invited too.

High profile gig. Don't even know what it's about, but I'm not around. Fancy going? You look like you need a drink, mate!"

Mark laughed.

Precisely, but Jonathan knew better than to rub his real needs under Mark's nose.

"I'll have a look," he said and grabbed the half-empty pack, the lighter and the mobile.

"Back in a minute."

Jonathan pushed the office door and walked along the empty corridor, up the small flight of stairs and through the narrow pathway that led him out of the Old Truman Brewery and onto Dray Walk, where those blessed with daytime freedom proudly paraded their carefree looking selves.

He lit up.

This girl was still asking him to make up his vodka-veiled mind about meeting her tonight, but, unfortunately, Jonathan wasn't used to making up his mind, vodka-veiled or not.

This was London, after all.

Where a burdensome past was constantly being eradicated and a future decided as you went along.

Where boundaries had stopped to exist and all constraints had long been blown away.

Jonathan had a deep drag.

This muddled collection of random streets and random souls didn't require anyone to make up anything.

That much was clear.

But something was nagging him. The nicotine mixed with the barbecue smoke of 1001 and a hint of lager from the Big Chill, all of which made for a tempting little teaser for the things to come, once he had survived this dreadful day spent pretending.

Something didn't let him go.

A couple of free drinks on a press event, and then?

To hell.

This wouldn't hurt anyone, would it? Cigarette in mouth, Jonathan started texting back.

Max took out his mobile and read the text message again. He looked up and had a deep breath.

This was it, wasn't it?

The George.

He shook his head.

This was it.

A dream he hadn't dared to dream all day, had come true. Max entered the courtyard and squeezed past those shivering through a frozen fag or a cheeky spliff. A fantasy that hadn't left his head, ever since Sarah's rushed goodbye from Café Evin this morning, had turned real, as his mobile had vibrated less than half an hour ago:

"I know this might sound a little spontaneous, but fancy popping around?"

This was all happening far too fast, but who was he to complain that she had asked him to meet her in a Dalston pub called The George, when that was exactly what he had secretly hoped for all day?

Max looked at the pub's sign again.

He had never cycled faster from Clapton to Dalston, the Round Chapel and St John flying past like shadows, as he had madly overtaken the 38, jumping the junction's red lights despite a higher principle not to do so, unless absolutely inevitable.

Leaving his domestic cage.

For this.

Temporarily leaving the battle.

For her?

He had spent all day squeezing his life, fine-tuned and tailored, once again, into a form that had looked more promising than any ever had.

Fired by this morning's encounter, Max had filled the wicked white boxes with more enthusiasm than ever before.

Max smiled.

He had clicked the submit button with a completely new kind of conviction that this, finally, was the one and there was no better way to celebrate than to meet the person that was waiting behind the door in front of him.

He pulled it open.

How should he start the conversation?

He stepped inside.

The warmth slapped his face, a dozen lively chats fighting a jukebox that was playing a Bowie song.

What could possibly happen?

Max turned his head, left, right, left, hectically scanning the tables for Sarah's face, but there was no sight of her.

"Max!"

She was standing right in front of him.

"So glad you came!"

At the counter?

"How are you?" Max said, even though the real question was a completely different one:

Who the hell was that guy next to her?

Even though the real question was this: who the hell was that girl on the other side?

She was just receiving the return cash for three shots of whatever, stupidly grinning at the other two and then at him, a polite introduction skipped to come straight to the point:

"Want one too?"

What the hell was going on here?

"Sorry Max," Sarah said.

Why wasn't she alone, just like Max had pictured all the way here, alternatives not even hiding at the back of his mind?

"Not at all," he said, trying to hide his disappointment behind a friendly face.

"So who are your friends?"

"We aren't friends," the girl in leggings said.

"Right," Max said.

"Okay, sorry, now..." Sarah said and pointed at the guy that had whispered into her ear the moment Max had entered.

"This is Jonathan," and:

"He isn't a journalist, but he likes to drink at press parties, especially if the beer is free."

"Nice to meet you, Jonathan."

Jonathan just nodded.

"And this is Lizzie, who is about to become an actress and is a friend of Jonathan, that's right isn't it?"

"Well," Lizzie said.

"Enough talk, boys and girls," Jonathan said, and:

"Let's drink these shots before –"

"You want one, Max?" Sarah said.

She was acting so unlike the Sarah he had met this morning.

"I'm okay, you go ahead," and, a little time-delayed:

"I'm in for the next round."

"That's the spirit," Lizzie said.

"Cheers, everyone."

"So, if you're not friends, how did you meet?" Max said, looking at Sarah, but a shot-fired Lizzie answered:

"Like people meet in this city."

Right.

Jonathan snorted.

"Just like that," Lizzie said.

Right.

"So, did you have a good day?" Sarah said. She was clearly more than tipsy.

Had that been the only reason for her text?

"Yeah, what did you get up to?" Lizzie said, as if they had known each other for ages.

"Well, I filled in an application form."

"Great stuff, man," Jonathan said, and:

"Anyone in for another round?"

"Sounds great," Sarah said to Max, and Max said, sounding not nearly as convincing as he wanted to:

"This one has to work out."

He was far too sober for this.

"Otherwise, I don't know..."

"An ultimatum!" Lizzie shouted and turned to the bar to order another four shots of whatever with the money Jonathan had just passed to her without a word.

"I like that," she said, and:

"I'll have one too, but I'm well on my way, I can tell you that. It's going to work out brilliantly. I've only just decided this, with a little help from this man here, but I've got the ball rolling big time already. I mean, it's all about knowing people and, honestly, if you're an artist, Hackney is really just a village."

"With a little more knife crime, yes."

Max looked at Sarah, but Sarah looked at Jonathan, because he said:

"So how about your boyfriend, Ms journalist? You were saying something."

"Was I?"

"He's in Berlin, isn't he?" Max said; he wanted to show these people that he knew Sarah better than they did, even though it wasn't true.

"Since this morning, yes," Sarah said.

"And here you are, drinking shots with three strangers," Jonathan said.

Sarah blushed a little.

"Hey, you kidnapped me from that PR party. I never intended to have more than one drink there and go home. I'm not usually..."

"You're quite the kidnapper, aren't you?" Lizzie said to Jonathan in a tone Max couldn't quite read.

What was this?

"Thanks for coming Max," Sarah said and turned away from Jonathan and Lizzie a little, splitting this gang in two.

Max took a few steps to the side.

"No, no, thanks for telling me, Sarah."

Looking into her face brought back the nervousness that had made him cover his coffee cup in sweat this morning.

"I really enjoyed our little talk at Evin, you know? It was... well, thanks so much for getting in touch."

"Sure. Did you make it to the office in time?"

"What? Oh yeah, sure, no problem. So you have great hopes in the application you sent today?"

Six sections, ten questions, two references.

"I have kind of staked my life on it," Max said.

Five times spell-checked and ten times fact-checked, this one had to end the battle, once and for all.

"If this one doesn't work out, then I don't know..."

"Hey you two splinters, what's the story?" Lizzie said from behind Sarah and pointed at another round of shots waiting on the pub's wooden counter.

"You guys are serious, eh?" Max said.

"It's the only way, my friend," Jonathan said and raised his glass, looking at them impatiently.

"To life," Lizzie said.

"Yeah, fuck life," Jonathan said.

"To us then," Lizzie said.

"To whom?"

"Whatever, to meeting," Lizzie said and Sarah smiled?

She raised her glass.

"To meeting."

She looked at Max, who finally unloosened the brown scarf that was still wrapping his neck.

"To 'just like that'", he said to the sound of four glasses, clinking together in their middle, and something happened the moment they did, a promise that couldn't be articulated enveloping the four of them as they were standing in a circle at the counter of a warm and noisy East London pub called The George on a Monday night in December, and everyone smiled, apart from Jonathan.

Lizzie tried to lift her heavy eyelids. Her dry mouth gasped for the water she had forgotten to bring to her mattress last night. She moved her shot-damaged head in slow motion. Outside, it was getting dark already; was that her mobile?

Shit.

She stretched her right arm, not moving the rest of her body, and grabbed the phone from the floor next to the mattress.

Shit.

A friend of a friend. A few strings, pulled; she had to get this, if she wanted to, or not, and she didn't.

"Hello?"

Lizzie coughed; this was the painful price for accepting red Marlboros in favour of her own rollies.

"Hi Lizzie, God, are you alright?"

"Yes. I'm fine, yes."

"It's Frieda here, honey, and I have good news for you."

Lizzie coughed again.

"The Arcola. Thursday at ten. You better be on time."

Lizzie tried to lift herself up.

"You're kidding."

"Most definitely not, honey. You're a lucky bee indeed. Doesn't happen too often, and especially not that quick."

"Wow, what can I say?"

"You could ask what the audition is about, for example. Listen, I don't have much time, they're looking for someone natural, someone who hasn't been through all the career actress stuff. Someone real. The character is an artist, so there you are. She's not really going anywhere, at some point she gives up, accepts nine-to-five and the lot, but they might cast someone else for that part, I think. For now, they just want someone who looks like a struggling artist and thinks like a struggling artist and there you are."

Lizzie couldn't speak.

"Quite promising if you ask me, but I have to run. As I say, try to be on time. Let's talk afterwards, okay?"

Lizzie couldn't think.

"Thanks, thanks so much, Frieda, I ...I..."

"Speak soon, honey."

A flash.

A blur.

A dream?

"Yes, speak soon."

A mad plan had just reached the point of no return and a bleary-eyed Lizzie slithered down her mattress again.

This was her role, wasn't it?

She closed her eyes.

This was Lizzie, wasn't it?

This was exactly what remained of her trip, open-eyed, stumbling into this madhouse with her lips too red and her skirts too short and her expectations blissfully unharmed, spending days, weeks, months, years just hanging out in front of 1001, moving from pasta salad to cans of Red Stripe, before busting The Redchurch closing time, only to end up, once again, eating 3am bagels with those that had no real home either.

Lizzie opened her eyes again.

This was exactly what remained of Lizzie, overdoing everything, rest assured that there was still plenty of time. That rushing and stressing was for other people.

Shit.

Her head was killing her, still top-level filled with a vicious brew of high-percentage poison.

Lizzie swallowed.

Still buzzing with far too much input; it was hard to say which really caused this hangover, a dazed blur intersected by flashes of conversation, every few seconds or so:

"So, can I call you Jo?"

"Only if I can call you Liz."

What had that been all about, her burning desire to spend another night of comfort with a stranger, crushed in front of her eyes, just because this guy knew no better than to snatch someone the same way he had snatched Lizzie.

Putting things into perspective.

Just because this guy had no respect whatsoever, denying Lizzie what she had longed for all weekend, to hand her what? Lunching class Sarah and would-be lunching class Max.

Hearing things like:

"So what's your work?"

As if Lizzie was like them.

As if Lizzie was a normal person, with a flat, and a job, and a boyfriend. With normal aspirations and normal dreams and not like her, running around like a nervous chicken, from one chance to the next. From one failed opportunity to another, not having a single answer to any of those embarrassing questions.

Getting this instead:

"Sweeping away hair? Really?"

If only Lizzie was a little bit more like them.

Settled and secure.

Settled and sorted.

Settled and safe and not shivering herself into another day of waiting, dreading nothing more than Christmas and all eyes on her and a tea spoon being twisted around again and again and again and no other sound, but her dad's heavy clock ticking in her back.

And ticking.

Lizzie threw away the blanket; what had that been all about, standing at the counter of her own local pub only to be told:

"You will be fine, Lizzie."

Just fine.

Just damn fine, hearing their stories while the one that had been the whole idea had just stood there, staring, drinking, staring. Not saying anything, unless it had concerned another round of drinks. Only acting half-way normal the moment Max and Sarah had started splitting off:

"So, Liz..."

She turned, slowly, and pushed herself into a precarious stand in the middle of her cold and dim room.

"So, Jo..."

He had left The George before any of them had even started thinking about calling it a night, leaving Lizzie no choice but to say:

"Okay, well, see you soon."

She took a few steps towards the window. The cold winter wind covered her naked legs in goose bumps. The colourful shine of the Christmas lights that lined the market now made it all the way up here. She wrapped her arms around herself and leaned her booze-heated forehead against the cold window.

She had an audition.

In two days' time Lizzie would step out of a small theatre on Arcola Street, having convinced those that were waiting for her inside.

Ready to convince the world.

In two days' time, everything would change, but right now all Lizzie wanted to know was if Jonathan would text again, so she could try, once again, to break through the wall he was keeping up around him.

She closed her eyes and kept them shut.

Sarah let her fingers glide over the soft, curved metal railings that lined the bridge. Down there, the Thames had already turned into a vague stretch.

A dark void.

A black mirror, reflecting whatever Sarah wanted to get reflected, seeing the scenes over and over again. Her mind was still in overdrive, even now, God knew how many hours later, processing thoughts it wasn't used to processing.

Index overflow.

No categories.

Sarah crossed her arms against the cold; this bridge led her towards the border of her box.

And the soldiers knew it.

She had acted on impulse, having survived the time between touching in and touching out without painkillers from her second drawer, because she didn't have painkillers in her second drawer any longer, a need taken by other routines. Having answered the suspecting questions posed by her colleagues with a shrug and a mumble:

"I just didn't sleep very well, that's all."

Sarah had acted, asking no one, boarding the wrong bus without even checking its destination. Eschewing the same streets, turns, junctions, for this breakout journey. Breathing a little deeper with every minute it had carried her.

Through unknown streets.

Past random houses.

Into dangerous terrain; the soldiers were loading their guns, because they heard Sarah repeat the evil words:

She was in charge.

Just like everyone.

Wasn't that the message she had taken from The George, striding home with a smile on her face?

The slogan that had vibrated through her head all day.

The truth that wouldn't leave.

Sarah placed her arms onto the railing. To her left, St Paul's cupola was wrapped in a misty grey. To her right, The Tate's rust-coloured chimney rose majestically into the South London sky, but the museum's brick elegance didn't conceal the dark clouds that were silently forming in its background.

Sarah looked up.

Something was brewing, there was no doubt; she pressed herself closer against the railing to fight the biting wind that was swishing past her back and heard Lizzie, all of a sudden:

"I mean, you've chosen it, right?"

Signing up the way she had.

Head high, riding on, five years and counting, not looking left and not looking right. In a city that was constantly leaning forward:

Only looking ahead.

"Or not?"

Two words and a carefree smile, as it was only managed by those that hadn't arrived yet.

"That's the way things go," and:

"You choose, baby."

And Jonathan had started nodding and Max had nodded, too, and all three of their freedom-spoilt faces had morphed into one determined, chiding long nod, which, God knew how many hours later, was still replaying in Sarah's head, as if in slow motion.

As if it wouldn't ever stop again until Sarah herself found the remote and pressed the button.

Sarah sighed.

She pushed herself up and started walking back; Peter would call in less than an hour, telling her about getting in and getting on and expecting her own little report, habitually framed by touching in and touching out.

Comfort in every syllable.

Assurance in every word.

Expecting the worn-out phrases that made up the full-colour picture as it was meant to look for someone like Sarah and for someone like Peter, rising undisturbed by sentences like:

"I'm not ready to give up my beliefs yet."

With fire in his eyes.

"I will fight this to the end, you know?"

With excitement pouring out of him, that had carefully touched Sarah before it had started wrapping her, a little more with every sentence Max had said.

"I'm a fighter, Sarah."

With a kind of pride in his voice that was reserved for those that actually had things to be proud of; why on earth was she allowing herself to think that much about a stranger?

Sarah walked quicker.

To her left and to her right, swarms of tourists passed her, starry-eyed, pointing at all the buildings they were seeing for the first time, her city spreading out in front of their night-programmed auto focus.

Everyone seemed to gaze at all those lights the same way Sarah once had, years ago, when she had just arrived, young and ready to go, before the months had flown by, year after year without a minute of reflection, because this city didn't allow reflection, unless you grabbed it with both hands, cancelling lunches and finding excuses and boarding the wrong bus to stare at the Thames while the drunken snippets from last night kept popping up.

This slow-burning thrill didn't want to leave.

Not even now, as she stepped off the bridge to board a box-bound return bus.

Her comfort zone in sight.

Had she really told Max that she wasn't even reading her own newspaper anymore?

That, once you were inside, you stopped being interested in the newspaper, because you were the one producing the newspaper and that, once you knew how the newspaper was produced, you even stopped believing in the newspaper.

Had it really all come out?

That, once inside, the childhood dream morphed into a dirty factory. With you on the conveyor belt.

Sarah crossed Queen Victoria Street.

The mobile phone in her left pocket vibrated; what was this stranger doing to her, showing her a perspective she hadn't even asked for?

Sarah stopped.

Opening windows for her she hadn't even known existed; Sarah took out her mobile and read the name she had hoped to read all day long and he was suggesting a walk somewhere and that was a wonderful idea, wasn't it?

She started smiling, even though the soldiers were shouting at her in a deafening unison.

This was it, wasn't it?

Nothing else could explain the rumbling that was besieging him from all sides.

Nothing else could explain this drone.

Jonathan tripped.

Nothing else could explain the rattling that left him without a chance to escape this killing field.

Surrounded.

Encircled.

Taken, his forehead covered in sweat, his T-shirt sticking to his pumping chest.

Jonathan was hit by another bass-punch to his stomach.

He squirmed.

In front of him, the bright lights were only waiting to deliver their fatal blow.

But Jonathan was still breathing.

In and out.

He was still moving as trained.

In and out.

He was still acting as drilled, not relying on a fallback, because there was no fallback, trapped between other bodies, naked warm flesh against his arms, his legs entangled with someone else's, tits against his shoulders, sweat on sweat.

Jonathan rocked forward.

And back.

The outcome of this war was in his hands, survival down to him, and Jonathan was still going strong, feeling others rub against him, as he floated through this crowd to clean himself from mistakes that should never have been made, his defences neglected with a terrible result:

What idiots!

Exposing him inside a pub the stray dog should never have come close to; the beats were hitting Jonathan.

And again.

He turned around.

And again.

What madness, conceding space to a laughable bunch of intruders, still trying to talk themselves into believing that togetherness was a help in their doomed attempts to find a place in this god-forsaken world; Jonathan tripped over his own feet and stumbled against another flouncing body, half-dead and done and through the small doorway that led into the front room.

For a shelter.

For a trench, the rattling kept at bay to rest for a few precious moments, his tingling back pressed against the backrest of a red armchair, clutching the half-empty pack of red Marlboros in his pocket.

What idiots, all three of them!

Jonathan needed a cigarette; he pushed his way past the swathes of incomers that were still streaming into this hellhole of a Shoreditch bar, expecting redemption. Hoping for sweet salvation from a dance floor that knew no rules, limits or shame. Longing for the sort of liberation that only a hellhole of a Shoreditch bar like this could provide:

Liberation on tap.

"Whatever," written on every wall.

Total abandonment was lying in the air and everyone in here played a part in whirling it up and around and straight into the bloody nostrils of those that were like Jonathan, desperate to inhale the sexed-up, lager-veiled perfume that was keeping them alive and here.

And how much he needed the fix tonight, having given in the way he had.

Jonathan pushed the black door leading to the staircase and stumbled down the filthy stairs.

His mind made the kind of comeback that only happened once you moved away from the action, leaving behind the sounds to be smacked by a night time wind, blowing up and down a deserted Old Street.

Jonathan stepped away from the door and dried some of the sweat on his forehead.

He lit up immediately.

This was the last resort, but so what? This world was going to the dogs and there was only today.

There was only right here.

There was only right now.

He inhaled.

There was only right here, right now, Tuesday night, Mother Bar.

A final straw.

Jonathan exhaled into the cold; Old Street looked as bleak and empty as it did on too many weekday nights. No one fried hot dogs on Hoxton Street. No one sold overpriced bagels opposite. No one stumbled in minicabs and no one stiletto-tripped down the kerb in front of him.

The dead bridge didn't echo laughter, or shouting, or anything, but the slow dripping of brown water from one of its rusty beams.

As heard a thousand times.

As if there had never been anything but this grey and lifeless stretch of overrated nightlife, where the light bulbs that wrote Electricity Showrooms had been switched off hours ago.

As seen a thousand times.

As if there had never been anything but this coke-fuelled crawl from Mustafa, Adem and Hakan to The Hoxton Bar and Kitchen. From Catch to The Macbeth, and back, leaving The Old Blue Last's trembling upstairs for the dark backroom of 333. Drinking up another last Stella inside The Foundry, just to tip-toe in the queue for On the Rocks, following suggestive skirts to the only places in this world where Jonathan could be himself, entirely.

He coughed.

Where his eyes would deliver a result, sooner or later, and send him boarding a shared minicab, holding hands and touching thighs, while his city passed in its familiar neon blur.

He coughed again.

Gasped.

Swallowed; where did these attacks come from, all of a sudden, hitting him out of the blue at least twice a day? He needed another drink to wash this down. Jonathan threw the butt onto the street. It died with a hiss in a puddle. Jonathan took a step towards it. The muddy water reflected his bleary face just like another had, a few weeks ago, when Jonathan had crawled along Hackney Road, too late for the kebab place and too late for Ye Old Axe and its mirrors and too late for another final drink anywhere, or a last, very last chance...

"Shut up," he mumbled.

When he had jumped into the puddle, just to feel something, and had jumped into every other puddle that had followed, all the way to his dark and empty flat.

"Shut up."

He turned around.

Thoughts like these couldn't be allowed, if you didn't want the shit to take over.

"So what's your love life like?"

Jesus.

Had Lizzie really asked that question?

Jonathan hastened up the stairs.

The black door opened and the sound grabbed him by the throat and put him straight where he belonged. Ready to fight this war until it was won.

That was what his love life was like.

"But Max, it's all so admirable, don't you see that?"

Sarah kept smiling as they entered Springfield Park through its open black metal gate. This was the location they had both agreed on yesterday night, four long days after Max had suggested this walk.

"Well, yeah, but..." Max said.

"It doesn't get you anywhere, does it?" he said.

"You, know, it's all nice and fine to have idealism, but it doesn't fit into any CV slot. It doesn't count as experience. It's not a skill."

Idealism was just another label.

"Yeah, but still..."

Idealism was just another word that had lost all its meaning in the muddle that went for life, these days, left-wing being right-wing. Male being female.

All being upside down.

"The thing is, you can have your idealism intact all the way to the grave, without ever giving it away. Without ever letting it slip. And in the end, you still haven't done a single thing in your life."

They started climbing up the hill that made up this East London stretch of green.

"Mhm," Sarah said.

As expected, Springfield Park was just perfect for their Saturday afternoon walk: little known, but romantically inclined, and close to his flat and not far from hers, yet miles away from both their normal lives.

Max had lost track of how many excited messages they had sent each other since The George.

Text by text, a little less formal.

Text by text, a little less distant.

"And then, I don't know, when you're dead and gone, they give you a cheap wooden cross or something in Highgate Cemetery or somewhere that just says: Max. Idealist."

Sarah laughed at the wittingly pompous tone in his voice.

"You know what the hard bit is?" she said.

How much he admired this woman.

Behind the cute white lodge at the hill's top, the sky was painted in a dull, ambiguous grey:

Things could go either way.

"The hard bit is to keep your idealism going, once you're inside. When everything is safe and secure and you start doing all these things you don't believe in anymore."

Sarah seemed to loosen up, a little more with every step they took up the hill.

"You know, I can't remember when I last wrote something for my newspaper because I believed it. That's just not what happens. Once you're in, it's very easy to forget the thing you initially wanted."

"Yes, well..." Max said.

Right now, all he wanted was to be picked up from the street and be allowed inside to join Sarah, who was everything he wanted to be.

Who had all he wanted to have.

"You know, it's quite easy to settle for the easy option. The first thing that comes around –"

"But isn't that what everyone expects?" he said.

As heard a thousand times from his mum and from his dad and from all those that took pleasure in lecturing him about his future as if it was theirs. Not understanding for a minute what was going on out here, where the rulebook was flowing down the drain.

Where the lights were about to go out.

"Yes, unfortunately that is what everyone expects," Sarah said and sighed a little.

For him, there was only one hope left and that was an application Max had polished, again and again, as if it was the only piece of work he was ever going to produce in his whole damn life, and only one outcome could still prevent Max from going wicked ways and that was victory, a letter that would end a battle that had lasted for far too long now, a casualty count a joke; when would they reply to him?

"The problem is that people are just so desperate to get in anywhere," Sarah said.

"Yeah, exactly."

They had almost reached the hill's top.

"And then you get in somewhere and you stop asking questions and that's that: you go along. You shut up. You shut down. You become like me, Max. Deeply afraid... of... of change."

She grabbed his arm.

"Any kind of change."

How much he fancied this woman.

"Sorry," she said.

"But no, what for?"

She looked at him; for letting out things that had probably been held hostage for far too long? She smiled at him. For leaving all undue restraint at the bottom of the hill, just the way Max had?

"Shutting up and shutting down. God, I have never talked to anyone about this, Max."

For words that felt like a long and dreamy kiss?

"Neither have I, Sarah," he said.

They turned around and the bare meadows gave way to a widescreen view over the forsaken marshes that spread in Hackney's east.

Max hesitated a moment.

A freight train rattled past in the distance. Bare masts dotted the empty landscape.

Then Max said:

"You could always quit, couldn't you?"

The grey sky had started turning dark. Another winter night was announcing itself. Max turned around and looked at Sarah, but Sarah, wearing an expression he couldn't read, didn't answer him.

Squeak.

Lizzie pulled along one treasure after another. Hanger for hanger, this was comfort in a sound.

Squeak.

Hanger for hanger, the tension left: a glittery black blazer.

Squeak.

A knitted blue sweater.

Squeak.

A green cardigan, skip, and a flowery summer dress, skip, and then this, pulled out immediately.

If nothing else changed, the clothes had to.

"How much is this one, honey?"

Only that, very soon, everything would change forever.

How great she had looked!

How confidently she had spoken the lines they had handed her and how lavishly they had praised her as she had stepped off the stage, ready to convince the world:

This was happening.

She had delivered a star performance on the Arcola's stage. Now, all she had to do was to relax.

"That's forty five, babe."

Now, all she had to do was to do the usual.

And that was to wait.

"It's gorgeous, isn't it?" the girl said. Lizzie turned towards her, oversized black glasses setting off an undersized green bodysuit. Lizzie fancied the small braces she used to hold her trousers. Lizzie fancied her ankle-high boots, too.

"Yeah, it is."

And if waiting was the only option, then waiting inside a warehouse designer studio was better than waiting inside her cold, damp flat.

"Want to try it on?"

If waiting was the only option, then shopping was the only answer, just like it had been for as long as anyone in this bare little room could remember, panicky news reports left to those that had no idea what this kind of life was all about.

"Yeah, why not," Lizzie said.

She carried the dress into the corner and pulled the thin curtain behind her.

"And what costume shall a poor girl wear," the Velvet Underground were singing from the small stereo on the floor.

"To all tomorrow's parties."

Lizzie couldn't get his smile out of her head.

She got out of her coat.

She couldn't stop seeing another two final Whisky Cokes being carried towards her, his pretty face shining in The Moustache Bar's mysterious blue light.

"Cheers, Liz."

Lizzie got out of her disintegrating Converse and stripped her frayed jeans skirt over her black winter leggings.

"Cheers, Jo."

No longer strangers, but friends?

She pulled her loose red t-shirt over her head and took the dress off the hanger.

No longer friends, but what, exactly, having spent a whole night hopping from one dark Dalston basement to the next, without either of them having to say a single word?

About another last drink.

About another last bar.

About another look into each other's eyes. Grabbing his arm to whisper:

"God, Jo, you don't even know how glad I am that I have met you."

Lizzie looked at her goose bumps in the mirror.

Had he really meant his quickly fired reply the way she wanted him to mean it?

She stepped into the dress and started buttoning up the front; it had taken five attempts, after all, to make him pick up his phone after The George, a dialling tone without a voice, again and again, until he had finally answered, on Wednesday night, responding to Lizzie's carefully worded request if he might, at some point, fancy meeting her for another drink with a gruff:

"Why not right now?"

The dress was gorgeous.

Lizzie turned around to see her back; how she had enjoyed being led away, once again, her hand placed in his and no decisions needed, until they had ended up, dance floor exhausted, eating 3am lentil soup inside a steamed-up Somine, where Lizzie had said so much less of what she had wanted to say. Where Jonathan had said none of what Lizzie had wanted him to say.

She started unbuttoning again.

Where it had all ended with a rushed hug; Jonathan had turned away as if he had suddenly realised that he had committed a terrible crime by granting her that night and had boarded a night bus and had left her behind without another word.

Lizzie got out.

Without another look; Lizzie put the dress on the hanger again.

Jonathan had left her without telling her again that she was made for acting and that it would all work out brilliantly, a glorious future in the making:

What if this was a terrible mistake?

She grabbed the dress and her coat and pulled the curtain; what if this would all end in failure again?

"I'll take this one," Lizzie said.

Filling the void with polyester satin.

This wouldn't end in failure. She knew that because Jonathan knew that.

"Great choice, babe."

"You take cards, don't you?"

Lizzie stepped closer towards her small table.

"Sure."

She typed in four digits to endure this torturous wait, no time frame given by those in charge, which meant that every hour was like a day now, until she would finally find out if she was to survive this Christmas and all eyes on her.

Or not.

"Cheers, honey."

Lizzie walked through the door and down the stairs, out of this cotton-scented sanctuary and onto Shacklewell Lane, where the cold air brutally grabbed what remained of her dreamy drift, feeling so close to someone who was so careful not to show what he felt.

Replaced, once again, by:

What if?

Replaced, once again, by:

What then?

Lizzie needed a hand, a crutch, Lizzie needed... a sudden vibration to her rescue?

She rummaged for her phone – when had the lunching classes started calling her, a number handed out without expecting consequences?

"Hi there," Lizzie said.

When had the lunching classes started asking exactly the right question at exactly the right time?

"How was the audition?"

"Sarah, it was amazing. Really, really good. I think I convinced them big time. It felt so good, I can't even tell you. Now I just have to wait, I guess."

Lizzie started walking.

"That sounds fantastic. Listen, I was just thinking... I don't know... Wouldn't it be nice to do something together again? I mean, I really enjoyed meeting you guys on Monday..."

Jo & Liz.

"Would you be up for dinner or something?"

"Sure," Lizzie said.

The more distraction, the better.

"Do you think your friend Jonathan would be up for it, too?"

"Yeah, definitely."

He had to.

"Great, I'll send around a message or something. Would Wednesday work for you?"

The sooner, the better.

"Any day works for me, Sarah. Forgotten? I have no other obligations but to wait."

"Sure, okay, speak soon then."

Lizzie turned around the corner. She pushed the mobile into her bag and grabbed the Golden Virginia. In front of her, the Christmas lights stretched towards a mist-veiled Gherkin, half-hidden by another monster in the making.

Lizzie filled a Rizzla.

Burning down either of those glass-and-steel beasts wouldn't be a crime, but the London Lizzie had chosen for herself wasn't down there, but up here, where Ali Baba was glaring in a reassuring way and the air was thick with the Turkish grill smoke that turned this corner into a twenty-four hour barbecue party.

Lizzie rolled.

How much she loved this city.

She licked and lit up; how much she loved the idea of becoming an actress.

Lizzie started walking, past the Rio Cinema's blue light, still switched off, towards her empty home; how much she had started loving someone who had to be told nearly as much and this dinner was Lizzie's chance, wasn't it? This dinner was all that counted now.

This was the edge of the box and the soldiers knew it.

"It's just myself," Sarah said.

She followed the waiter to a small table for two and put her bag on the empty chair opposite.

The soldiers closed ranks.

"Thanks," she said.

The soldiers loaded.

Sarah smiled the smile of a professional woman going for a late lunch, only this was Church Street, Stoke Newington.

Only this was Monday, 4pm.

Only Sarah hadn't touched in and wouldn't touch out, a whole day taken off, no questions asked.

She leaned back.

There was no on else inside the restaurant. The small room seemed even darker than usual. Around Sarah, all serviettes were untouched. You could hear the clatter of cutlery from the kitchen.

"Are you ready to order?"

This was between Sarah and Sarah.

"Yes."

She had a quick look at the menu, but Rasa's offering was familiar from a dozen nights when the professional couple had deemed cooking impractical, their usual dinner conversation outsourced to these kitschy pink tables.

"I'll have Vangi, please, Kayia and Nadan Paripu. And Pappadavadai as a starter, please."

Not considering a second opinion.

Permission not needed.

"Sure," the waiter said and Sarah added, asking no one but herself:

"And a glass of white wine, please."

The soldiers flustered.

The soldiers stiffened.

But the waiter just said:

"Sure."

The soldiers were twitching the sleeves of Sarah's jumper, but Sarah just smiled.

"Thanks," she said.

Sarah simply pushed them away, gently but determined. Carefully, but leaving no doubt whatsoever.

That this was Sarah, taking charge.

That this was Sarah, standing up.

That this was Sarah, confronting a bunch of uniformed losers that had shouted orders at her for far too long now.

She straightened up.

She almost laughed at their clumsy attempts to assert their waning authority.

Was it really that easy?

The army in her head started behaving just the way Max had said they would: the soldiers were putting their arms on their legs to gaze, sullenly, at their boots.

The waiter brought the wine and Sarah had a quick sip.

"What a wonderful walk," Max had texted on Saturday, just as Sarah had finished her sanitised version for Peter:

"Everything's fine here."

Just as Sarah had made her plan to get them all together again.

Oh, Max.

Oh, wondrous master of a trick that could melt her professional mask, ever so cool and confident, into the kind of warm and uncontrolled smile that was trying to take over her face again right now.

Oh, Max, who had been right all along: there was a life without touching in, wasn't there?

Sarah had another sip.

There was not standing where the Stoke Newington office shuttle stopped, picking up those with early morning thoughts and their hair still wet.

There was avoiding the same streets, turns, junctions for this; roaming the streets of her neighbourhood without a purpose.

Without a plan.

Without anyone telling her anything, taking turns as they had popped into her head, destination-less drifting past dingy pubs and betting shops, from Café Z to Clissold Park. Out of The Blue Legume and into the Stoke Newington Bookshop, where Sarah had just bought her first novel in years.

She reached over the table.

All day, she had seen another world, the usual game replaced by a deep breath.

She took out her mobile.

All day, her box had grown bigger.

And bigger.

There was no message. She had a confirmation from everyone, but Jonathan, who had simply ignored her carefully worded attempt to re-unite four random souls.

To flirty words.

To excitement.

To Sarah having the time of her life, because three strangers were stirring things up.

Sarah placed the mobile on the table.

Peter would call any minute now and expect their usual office-to-office check-in, but she would worry about a suitable excuse for not being where she was meant to be when it actually happened, the canteen playing Indian ambient music because it was running a curry-themed week, or something.

She smiled.

Everything led there, didn't it?

Everything Max had told her pointed in one direction and, slowly, Sarah was turning her head there.

Slowly, Sarah approached.

Slowly, Sarah was getting ready to tackle a fear that was still being quenched, morning after morning, by touching in and was kept at bay, having touched out, by a straight journey into her comfort zone and another dinner table conversation that stayed exactly where it was meant to stay. Not for a moment touching what a professional women wasn't meant to touch:

The foundation.

Life's holy base.

The waiter brought a small basket with the crunchy, small pappadoms.

"Can't wait for Wednesday," Max had texted yesterday. And neither could she.

"xx."

"xx."

Everything pointed there, didn't it?

Everything pointed at confronting a worry that had started to creep in not so long after they had given her a desk, a phone, a life, and had grown, without her properly noticing, day by day by day, touching in and out and in and out and in and out.

Until, at some point, it had taken over.

The soldiers were half asleep by now, but Sarah knew that they would wake up, sooner or later.

That shutting them out was only a temporary measure.

She shuffled on her chair, forward and back; everything led there, didn't it?

She could see herself walking in.

She could see herself speak.

She could see herself walk out again, not looking back; Sarah shuffling forward.

Everything pointed at finally dealing with an unease that, five years in, was still being treated with another excuse.

She shuffled back.

How much longer would she be able to deny that the box was choking her?

Forward.

That the soldiers prevented her from living the life she was meant to live?

And back.

How much longer would she still be able to lie to herself? Sarah shuffled forward again:

There was no other way, was there?

She had to kill.

Tick.

Tick.

Tick towards tomorrow, when Max would finally be able to say all he needed to say about an understanding he didn't understand and a magic he couldn't describe and a feeling he didn't dare to name, not even to himself:

Mangal at 8.

Nothing was more important than this dinner, not even the news he had received a few hours earlier, a huge pile of monochrome screens up for recycling and a small door off Shoreditch High Street, closed forever.

Leaving Max, standing outside.

Leaving Max, finally, fully and officially unemployed, because someone else was dictating the action now.

Max sighed.

The battle had just turned violent.

He put his hands in his pocket.

Around him, there were trees, but no leaves, football pitches, but no one to play on them. He stared down the forsaken pathway that crossed the park. At its end, two blue commuter trains crawled past each other:

Out of the city, into the city.

As if there was movement.

When there was only standstill, another dull chapter in the story of Max, the idealist, sitting on a lonely park bench on Hackney Downs to keep doing what he had been doing all his London life and that was to wait.

Wait.

Wait.

In the far distance, the glittering lights of the City fooled those willing to be fooled into believing that the powerhouse was still alive, when the powerhouse was long dead; Max pressed his back against the bench:

Something terrible was going on.

His phone started ringing.

Out there, the world was changing in a way no one had ever seen, but none of it made any sense at all.

Max looked at the display.

Tick.

Tick.

Tick towards the end of another call spent ignoring the same old question, because there was still no answer.

"Mum, have you forgotten what I told you?"

"I just thought..."

"Yeah, well, there is no news. There you go. Does it feel better to hear it from me?"

Almost beaten.

"I'm sorry..."

Did it feel better to hear him hiding the battle's ugly face for a fake sense of peace?

"It's alright," he said and pressed his back a little harder against the bench he was sitting on.

What was the point, telling her about the call centre slamming its door into his face?

What was the point, telling her anything, a sheltered inside clashing with an outside that was getting crueller by the day?

"Alright, son."

A long distance call, where all the understanding was lost along the way.

"Alright."

Where every word they uttered only increased his despair and every word he uttered only increased their disappointment, his parents being like all parents, filled with an expectation that had been proven, again and again, by every generation.

Except theirs.

That had been true for every decade, but this:

That their children would do better.

"I'll call you when there is any news, okay?"

Max pressed red; the certainties his parents were still taking for granted had started rising towards this dark December sky as one big cloud of smoke, but they kept thinking: then. When this had long become:

Now.

Max shuffled; and now, even those that, until recently, had still harboured ambitions to be fished out of this pressure cooker city called London, were slowly giving in.

Now, even those that, until recently, had still entertained a vague hope that someone would stir this mad brew again so they could perhaps rise, just a little bit, closer to the top and be seen, were screaming:

Surrender.

Now, there wasn't even a chance anymore, a million future plans being crossed, slashed, destroyed: This battle was escalating beyond anyone's wildest dreams and, all around Max, people were no longer just floating.

But drowning.

All around him, people were no longer just struggling, but fighting for their bare survival, and here, on a lonely park bench on Hackney Downs, was Max.

Still chasing his dream.

He shook his head.

He pushed his hands into his pocket and took them out again and pushed them in again.

Would he sit next to or opposite Sarah?

He could stage another replay of the same old story, criss-crossing his adopted home turf to bear the waiting, from Stamford Hill to Upper Clapton, passing the mysterious marshes only to end up, none the wiser, exactly where he had started.

But it wouldn't help.

He would still be imagining Sarah whisper these words into his ear:

"Fancy coming to mine after this?"

He would still be imagining himself nodding.

And nodding.

And nodding; Max jumped up and started walking without any idea where to walk to.

"Anyway, I'm so glad that you all made it, in the end..."

Sarah looked at him.

The open grill fire was turning Mangal into a hot house even here, right next to the restaurant's front window, where it was, as agreed, Max opposite Sarah.

Lizzie opposite him.

Hiding was impossible and for the last two hours Jonathan had been strangely calm about it, his defences relaxed by whatever was lulling this particular table of theirs, but now it was building up:

"Yeah, yeah, blah blah..."

These people were strangling him.

"What's that supposed to mean?"

For the last two hours, he had tolerated what had happened at this particular table of theirs, where every single word spoken had seemed to underline what didn't need one more word of underlining, but was still getting underlined sentence after sentence after sentence:

Some people had found what they had been looking for.

He had tolerated the ridiculous sparkle that had taken over the eyes of Max the moment he had taken his seat and the childish smile that hadn't left Sarah's face ever since; he had tolerated the constant stare he was getting from Lizzie.

But, now, what had been merely bubbling was coming out in full five-pint glory:

"Blah. Blah. Blah," he said.

"Hey, just because you're bored doesn't mean you have to spoil this for the rest of us," Max said, but before Jonathan could say anything, Lizzie said:

"I don't think Jonathan is spoiling anything for anyone by stopping you two from flirting like that."

"Excuse me?"

These people were choking him.

"Nothing. Keep flirting, what do I care?"

He had a large sip from his beer. These people were pushing him into a corner with their newly-found happiness; these people were eroding his base, but something prevented him from just getting up.

Something prevented the usual escape.

"Anyone up for another drink, then?" he said and looked at their over-excited faces.

"I think we're all still fine. Quite a drinker, aren't you?"

"Well..."

His defences were out of order.

"I'll have another one with you," Lizzie said and had a large sip from her beer, still nearly full.

"I prefer talking to drinking," Max said and looked at Sarah, but Sarah looked at Jonathan, exploding:

"Jesus!"

"What?"

"Talking, eh? Have you even listened to your own non-stop talking in the last two hours?"

"What do you mean?"

"I mean all of you."

"What's that supposed to mean?"

Clinging to each other as if there were no other people in this world, but those sharing this window table.

"Forget it," Jonathan said.

"Just because you don't give a shit about anything doesn't mean we can't have a conversation, does it?"

A life, lived-as-you-go.

Over and out.

What idea did they have?

"That's not fair, Max," Lizzie half-shouted, but Jonathan didn't say anything.

Jonathan just looked at his glass of beer.

"Not Jonathan's fault that you care too much about everything, is it?" Lizzie said, and:

"Hasn't exactly brought you far, has it? Or anywhere at all."

But Max didn't answer.

"Lizzie," Sarah said.

"Sarah," Lizzie said.

They looked at each other.

"Don't you even get started with stuff working out eventually or some shit. I'm sure Max is as sick of hearing that word as I am. Anyway, fucking eventually isn't very believable from someone who never had to bother with it."

"Hey, that's not true."

"No? Well, when have you ever been required to stay motivated?"

"I'm... Anyway, you don't even know."

"What?"

"You know, I'm about to, tomorrow..."

Jonathan looked at her.

There was something in her eyes, excitement and nervousness in a wrestle.

"What?"

"Cut it, Lizzie," Max said, and:

"Sarah doesn't need that kind of crap from you. Anyway, when have you ever fought for anything?"

Lizzie didn't answer.

"And now you're trying to become an actress without even knowing anything about the theatre, is that it?"

"What?"

"You still haven't told me what kind of plays you like."

"No I haven't. What is this, a job interview?"

"I doubt you've ever been to one..."

"God, I wish no one had invited you, Mr Perfect."

"Hey, I did the inviting and I have invited Max and you and Jonathan, anyway..."

"Yeah, great idea, eh?" Jonathan said.

"Why don't we just try to be peaceful?" Sarah said and half-resumed the child-like smile she had worn all evening.

"Yes, exactly," Max said; you had to be blind not to see how much he fancied Sarah.

"All hail to peace, then," Jonathan said and raised his empty glass towards three full ones in a half-intended attempt to finish what he had started, words having spluttered without control.

"Peace, eh?" Lizzie said, and:

"Suppose that's very easy for you guys, isn't it?"

"What?"

"I mean, you don't have to fight very much to get through this goddamn life, do you? You don't have to spend all day waiting and shivering and praying that something works out fucking eventually because for you it already has."

"What's that supposed to mean?"

"What I just said."

"Do you have any idea, Lizzie?" Max said, and:

"Do you have any idea?"

And then:

"Have you ever heard about the battle?"

"My fight."

"The soldiers."

"This war."

And then:

Silence.

Jonathan hastily finished his beer and placed the empty glass on the table in front of him.

Max twisted his fork.

Sarah played with her earrings.

Lizzie moved her zip.

Up.

And down.

Up.

And down.

As if they hadn't just shouted what they had shouted at each other, loud enough for all the tables around them to hear every word:

One like all.

As if this hadn't happened:

All like one.

What the hell had happened?

Jonathan turned his glass.

Max placed his hands on his lap.

Sarah placed hers on the table.

What the hell...

Lizzie stopped the zipping, grabbed the menu from the table's middle and said:

"Who's up for a desert?"

They all looked at her. No one said a word.

"Actually, I think I'm going to go," Lizzie said and got up and looked at him.

Jonathan looked down into glass.

She kept looking.

"I'm going too," Sarah said next to him and Max, without a second's delay:

"I'll come with you."

They both got up and put on their coats and put their twenty pound notes next to the one Lizzie had just left and Sarah said, head turned at him:

"Jonathan?"

But he kept looking down.

"Well, see you," someone said, but Jonathan didn't look as they disappeared, one after the other, through the restaurant's door and out and away to keep wallowing in whatever this was, because they still didn't get it, did they?

This was London.

Jonathan rushed up. This was the twenty first fucking century.

Everyone was meant to fight alone.

Wasn't that still true?

Lizzie still didn't understand what had happened yesterday. It still didn't make sense, the way they had said what they had said at that restaurant table. The way they had, for just a short moment, seemed so close; closer than she had ever felt to anyone.

Lizzie shook her head.

The way they had seemed deeply connected as the words had just poured out.

None of them could have been in control at that moment; none of them could have been in charge, but that didn't help her make sense and it did fuck all to brush away what had just happened in her shitty flatshare in shitty Dalston in the shitty life of Lizzie, the shitty artist:

Fuck.

She smashed the can against the white wall opposite her; it just happened.

Fuck.

There it was, a small stain of warm Stella on an otherwise empty canvas.

Fuck.

The beer started running towards the dusty floor of her room; the can didn't move.

"Hey, what happened?" Amanda screamed from the kitchen.

"Nothing," Lizzie mumbled.

Nothing had happened and nothing would happen.

There it was.

"Hey, Lizzie! What the hell happened?"

"Nothing!"

"It didn't sound like that."

"Just leave me alone, Amanda, okay?"

She rushed up and slammed the door; there was only one person she wanted to talk to right now, but that person wasn't picking up the phone.

She slumped onto her mattress again.

Where was Jonathan, now that she needed him more than ever?

Three words like a knife.

A sentence like a stab.

Lizzie pulled her laptop towards her and clicked away the tyranny of a so-called social network that was expecting the same half-lies her parents were waiting for, but Lizzie was sick and tired of feeding the greedy monster:

The only status update she had to offer to anyone was another question mark.

Lizzie clicked.

She scrolled up and down her play list, but nothing excited her and once again it felt as if life was nothing but a comeback: from those bands to everything advertised in the fashion magazines that were piling in the corner, everything signalled the end and nothing a beginning, because that was the age and that was Lizzie, who was part of it.

Because she wasn't coming up with anything either.

Lizzie clicked.

In front of her, a lifetime of music reorganised itself. Names were giving in to numbers that reduced a whole year to four digits.

Lizzie scrolled into her childhood.

Oh, to return to that small bedroom, where, cosy and cushioned, she had spent hours and hours wondering what it would feel like to become an adult, trying to make sense of lyrics that, then, hadn't made any sense at all, mumbled verses about broken hearts and broken dreams and yet another up-beat chorus about all those crazy nights spent in the bars of the big city.

Oh, to be there again, soaking up words that had heralded a time to come and a future to be made, as they had started their glorious stride into this city.

Overdoing everything.

But now, Lizzie was right in the middle of it, leaning against the bare wall in a freezing room, spending her nights with a stranger that had stopped being one, her vulnerable heart in his careless hands and another broken dream in hers. Another broken fucking dream on the floor; she still couldn't believe what had happened a few minutes ago.

Lizzie skipped a track.

Oh, to have those choruses back and deny that the soundtrack was a different one now, having tried and having failed, once again, slithering on without a fight, just because life was like that:

You chose.

To be an artist.

To be an actress; Lizzie grabbed the can of Stella from its puddle on the floor and started squeezing it, slowly, until the small cracks started crazing her hand.

You chose.

To be.

It was the century's preferred religion, hammered into hurting heads by smiley-faced missionaries on every billboard.

From every bus:

Choose, or drown.

It was the modern world's fetish of choice, haunting people wherever they went.

Choose, or die.

The deadly disease no one had diagnosed yet.

"Lizzie, sweetheart," Pedro said outside of her door.

"What is it, arsehole?"

"Whoo..."

"Leave me alone, okay? I'm not feeling well. If you're bored, why don't you fix the toilet seat?"

"Bad day, eh?"

"Bad life, more like...fuck, go away," and:

"My door's closed for a reason."

"Alright, alright...just wanted to hear if you wanted another beer or something. I'm popping down to–"

"Yes, actually."

One comfort left.

"See? Got you covered, sweetheart. Just lay back and relax and all will become good."

Why was every person in this world telling her that everything would become good, except those that had been meant to tell her just that, but had opted for something else instead, without even so much as warning:

"We are sorry."

Without even a chance for Lizzie to raise her arms and scream in defeat the way she was used to, having picked up their call all too confident that there had been no need for a shield.

A cover.

A preparation to run off the way she had done so many times before.

"We are sorry."

Had they any idea what they had been doing, casually taking away her last resort?

Her final chance.

Lizzie grabbed her mobile.

"Where are you, Jonathan?"

There was no longer a point in denying that Lizzie needed him, not after Mangal and whatever had happened there, but all she got in return for that brave admission was a dialling tone, and that left her with no choice but to dial a different number and say:

"Hi Sarah."

And hear:

"Lizzie, hi, listen I can't really talk right now, I'm just... I'll call you back okay, I'm –"

"Don't bother."

"What's the matter?"

"Nothing."

"You sound a bit..."

"I'm fine, I just thought...nothing. Take care."

"I'll call you tonight, okay? There will be something to celebrate, I'm about to make sure there is... I'll tell you then, and perhaps we can celebrate your new role too, what do you think? Any news?"

Lizzie just let the phone drop. The battery case popped open, choking Sarah, choking Lizzie.

Dumping everyone that strangled her.

"We are sorry."

Lizzie pulled the blanket over her head and rolled up like a hedgehog.

Had she really squandered her final chance?

"Mum, really, just leave me alone, okay?" Max said, sitting in the corner of a dimly lit pub around the corner from his Clapton flat.

She was the last person he needed now.

"But Max, don't you see –"

He still hadn't made sense of Mangal yesterday.

"You know, you haven't got a clue, Mum! You have no idea what's going on out here."

He still hadn't made sense of what had happened on a couch inside a Stoke Newington flat.

"But we told you not to be so stubborn and look for other things and –"

"You told me nothing."

He still hadn't made sense of an email that had arrived a few hours earlier.

"We... Max, Dad wants to talk to you –"

"Yes, but I don't want to talk to Dad or to you or to anyone. Just leave me alone, for fuck's sake."

He pressed red.

The tears didn't flow down his cheeks, but just stood there, in his eyes, as if waiting.

As if there was anything left to wait for.

He had a large sip from the pint of Guinness that was standing on the table in front of him and rubbed his eyes; he hadn't seen it.

It hadn't happened.

The email had never arrived.

Max hadn't seen it, just as everyone was constantly pretending not to have seen violence on buses and racism in the press:

There was no setback.

There was no failure.

Just as everyone was constantly denying that the fighting was about to begin, over the last drop of oil and the last bucket of water and the last piece of cod swimming in the oceans surrounding the dreary landmasses that were occupied by six point seven billion people in constant denial:

Things weren't slipping.

Things were fine.

Things were absolutely marvellous and Max had never received the email ending with very best wishes for a so-called future.

He had another sip.

As if the rejection he had received in response to his application was the real problem; he looked at the mobile lying in front of him. What had happened inside Mangal was still a blur, but what had followed on her couch was much clearer than Max wanted it to be now:

"You want ice with that, Max?"

"Just come here and I'm happy."

"So nice to have you here."

"So nice to be here..."

The image refused to go, his leg touching hers as Sarah had sat down next to him, putting a final drink on the table in front of them, just the way she had carefully suggested, following what had seemed like an hour of tip-toeing indecision on Stoke Newington High Street.

"You know what I mean, Max? It seems unfamiliar, but so very familiar at the same time."

The scene replayed again and again, his nervous reflection in Sarah's large mirror and a folk-type band to fill the silence. Thoughts that had overtaken each other, one killing the next before it had been able to emerge properly, and a polished speech that had remained undelivered, because excitement and uncertainty had continued to battle it out, not delivering a winner.

"I... I feel exactly the same, Sarah."

The image simply refused to go, his leg touching hers again, as they had both put their empty glasses on the table, carefully re-adjusting their positions only to gin-fired forget the kind of flinching that came by instinct, usually.

Shuffling, once again, but not away from each other, but closer; there, finally.

Closer.

And then...

Max had a hasty sip; in the end no one had been hurt, so why wasn't Sarah picking up his calls?

Max looked around the wood-panelled room.

In front of him, three students were having the kind of intelligent conversation that had made him make The Elderfield his local the moment he had arrived in Clapton:

Another clueless incomer.

Another face in this crowd.

Next to them, a smiley-faced couple were playing a board game. Neil Young was quietly singing a tune he didn't recognise; a small Yorkshire Terrier was strolling around. In this corner, there was only Max and his growing silence.

"I don't think that's a good idea," had been the end of it.

"I'm so sorry," had been the end of it, hadn't it?

Max finished the Guinness.

He had just swallowed what had been pretty much his last remaining money, all hope to ever change his situation wiped out by another smug Kaiser of the inside having decided, feet on a table, not to take this particular life any further at this stage.

And now?

Now, the fragile construct he had created with Sarah in the last few days was swaying in front of his eyes, ready to collapse just the way the towers had and then the banks.

Max turned his empty glass.

Here was the problem:

Sarah could just go back.

Sarah could simply return to a reassuring desk and a loving boyfriend and pretend that nothing had ever happened, not Evin or The George, not Springfield, Mangal or the couch.

That was the injustice.

Sarah could simply put her worries were she had always kept them and forget the smiles and the words and the understanding and turn back to the main road, where the signs were familiar and everything was just fine, only that, for Max, there was no main road.

His breathing slowed to a flat snort.

Only that, for Max, there was only the wriggled mean little path that had just ended with a towering dead end T; didn't Sarah understand that, for Max, this hadn't been just another journey, but the only journey possible?

His breathing became a weak whine.

He picked up the phone from the round table in front of him and switched it off.

Here was the problem:

Sarah was finished with him, time enjoyed; time to move on, and she could simply return to everything Max would never have and there was nothing he could do about it.

He pushed himself up.

The brutal truth sank in as he stumbled away from connections that filled this pub with an energy he wasn't likely to regain, through the narrow door and onto the cold and empty streets of this residential no-man's-land, where his breathing slowed down even further.

The brutal truth was sinking in:
Sarah would just go back.

The soldiers were dead!
Sarah couldn't stop smiling.
The box was open!
Her freedom had been returned and Sarah smiled and smiled as she toddled through the Stoke Newington street that housed her comfort zone.
She was free!
Sarah squinted.
From all sides, the light was coming in, even though nightfall had long started covering the city.
From all sides, this glare was hitting her.
She closed her eyes.
The soldiers were gone. There wasn't a single one left; there was no doubt.
She opened her eyes again and felt her way along the neighbour's front wall, her numb fingers gliding over the cold stone, seam for seam for seam.
She had acted, asking no one.
She had done it.
Sarah walked up the small flight of stairs that led to her front door and fumbled for the keys.
How silly they had looked, raising their shaky hands in defeat, in the middle of the open-plan office. Pleading for mercy, which Sarah hadn't been willing to grant.
She dropped the keys.
She had single-handedly killed the army in her head; Sarah picked up the keys and opened the door, but not even her dark flat could stop a shine that was brighter than anything she had ever seen. Sarah glided out of her coat and dropped it to the floor behind her. In the living room, the mirror looked at her as if it knew everything already.
She took a step towards it.
"So," she said and smiled, but the person looking back at her wasn't Sarah at all, was it?
"So," Sarah said again and allowed herself to slide down the armrest of her couch and squeezed her cold hands between her wide-legged black trousers. She had left the desks, just as imagined, striding past row after row, not looking back.
Not turning around.

She had left the blank faces and the disbelief and the puny poses of those that hadn't understood a thing and she had never felt better.

Her shrewd strategy had been implemented.

The daring plan she hadn't mentioned to anyone, not even to Max, not even yesterday, not even on this couch, had been executed with a smug shrug:

There would be no more touching in and there would be no more touching out.

Sarah closed her eyes, but the semi-dark curtain that came as a result didn't do much to keep away the flashes that had started the moment she had boarded the afternoon 149, home-bound, but half-empty, making its way, machine voice-guided, through the same streets.

The same junctions.

The same turns.

Sarah ripped open her eyes; nothing would ever be the same again.

Sarah grabbed the armrest.

A shiver ran down her spine and started spreading...

Sarah rushed up, but it had seized her.

She hastened to the kitchen and grabbed a glass from the sink and filled it with water and started sipping herself towards a little more clarity.

Towards a little more calm in her veins, where the bubbling had grown with every shot she had fired, but, now, wouldn't stop.

Sarah sat down on a kitchen stool, but got up again immediately, placed the empty glass on the sink and turned towards the living room, where the mirror laughed at her.

"What do you know?"

Sarah walked back to the couch and leaned against the armrest. What was happening to her focus?

So sharp.

So clear.

So strong for days, having only seen what she had wanted to see: this, her final aim.

She pressed herself against the leather.

What was happening to her mind?

So calm.

So determined.

So sly for days, having heard everyone say the same thing, again and again. A chant that couldn't have been mistaken. A chorus that had propelled Sarah here, surrounded by bodies that were bleeding because Sarah had decided so.

She rushed up.

The box was open.

She turned hot and cold and hot again.

The box was gone.

The room started spinning, the mirror and the couch became one, two, one, two, one. Sarah walked towards the bedroom door. She rested against the frame, briefly, breathing in and out, before she entered the bedroom to take off her low-heeled shoes, without an idea at all what was happening to the veil that had settled over her the moment the magic had started, only a few days ago.

So soothing.

So sweet.

So lulling for days, having kept away everything that hadn't underlined this, the biggest adventure of her life, Peter and her parents to be informed later and Max to be filled in over a glass of wine and a proud smile as soon as yesterday's excitement had given way to a realisation that kissing wasn't part of this special relationship.

A step to be praised.

Sarah got out of her blazer jacket and let it drop behind her.

Her masterstroke.

She stripped away her trousers and unbuttoned her shirt; what was happening to whatever it was that had wrapped her so nicely and all the way here? She dropped the shirt and took a few steps forward.

Here she was, totally exposed.

She threw away the blanket and slipped underneath, pretending to feel safe in a comfort zone that was losing all its comfort.

Here she was, totally vulnerable?

She pulled the cold blanket all the way to her face, but there was no point. She had acted and this was the result.

She closed her eyes.

She pressed the cold blanket against her shivering body as hard as she could, but it didn't prevent this dizzying realisation from growing:

This, now, was just herself.
This was it:
This was the outside.

Jonathan leaned against the sticky steel counter. Around him, they had given up already, broken cowboys on stools, speechlessly staring into their half-empty glasses as if there were any answers in there, but Jonathan wasn't prepared to follow their lead.

"Can I have a kiss as well, please?" he said to the short-haired, big-breasted waitress serving him.

Because the desire didn't leave:

His lips touching someone else's; someone else's tongue touching his.

"Come on..." he said.

That strange moment inside Mangal yesterday had been the beginning of something he just couldn't get this sleepless, drunken, messed up head around.

"What?"

She tried to sound snappish, but it only made her sound even more sexy.

"Nothing," he mumbled.

She didn't look at him, not for a second.

"Nothing..."

Jonathan downed the first bottle in the time it took her to get his return cash.

"Thanks," he said.

Another fake princess without a bra. Another lovely human being that rejected the stray dog with a shrug.

"Who's next?" she said.

But not to him.

Jonathan turned away from the counter and looked into the neon light that was meant to kill, once and for all, what he had been trying to kill ever since he had been forced to stare at his broken defences on a restaurant table in front of him, while, on the other side of the window, vague, untouchable shadows had turned a rainy street into a painful slideshow of disconnection, prompting this totally unfamiliar doubt...

It had worked so well, hadn't it?

It had worked so beautifully, caring for no one, but himself, modern life's only logical consequence; Jonathan had a large sip from his second bottle and crossed the dimly lit dance floor that was supposed to finally finish a feeling he just couldn't point his finger at.

It had worked so brilliantly, hadn't it?

Jonathan carried himself into the dark, little corner next to the speakers that were meant to drown, once and for all, a feeling that was eating him up.

"Come on," he said, but something was about to go down and it didn't help to recall all those times he had seen his trilby-hat-wearing self in these mirrors, flouncing on whatever they had sold him at the bottom of the piss-and-sweat staircase across the room from here. Moving to lure and score and forget whatever had to be forgotten as he had looked at the only person in this room that could be trusted.

"Come on, boy."

He had another three large sips from his beer, but he wasn't really getting there, even though he had spent all of last night surrounded by the same debris and dust that had nearly killed him last week. But this time his body hadn't begged for sleep as he had zombie-crawled up a late morning Kingsland Road; this time his body had asked for something Jonathan still hadn't found.

Despite The Dove.

Despite The Dolphin.

Despite the food-steamed, group-fucked Cat and Mutton, where the stray dog had been the only person standing.

Despite The Haggerston.

Something was happening to him since Mangal had delivered a moment he still couldn't explain, for just a second; the intense sense of a connection, cruelly rammed into his defenceless self, somewhere far too deep...

Jonathan had a hasty sip.

Where even he was vulnerable?

"Damn it."

Not even the wanking had worked the way the wanking was supposed to work, delivering reaction, satisfaction, peace: Jonathan had spent what had felt like an hour trying to squeeze every inch of desire from a wrinkled little penis this afternoon, only to be left feeling exactly the way he had before, not having silenced these voices, but having handed them a fucking megaphone.

Louder than Jaguar Shoes.

Louder than Zigfrid.

Louder than the fucking Russian Bar?

Jonathan finished the bottle.

All was under control.

Everything was fine.

In front of him, the stage was set and the show was about to start exactly the way it had a hundred times before and that was all he needed, wasn't it?

The mirror-walled arena that had rescued him a thousand times already was right in front of him and all he had to do was to reach the click and go, but instead he coughed, because cigarette cues were no longer needed for attacks that grabbed him by the throat.

Jonathan leaned against the speakers for support.

He coughed again.

How many times had he stifled the warning voices, so loud and clear, in favour of another treacherous hiss to find another beer, bar, bed and cheers and on?

How many times had he ignored the signals?

But the dance floor was filling!

A pair of leather leggings had started moving rhythmically next to a pair of skinny jeans and he wanted nothing more than to let go and jump in.

But he couldn't.

Jonathan started shaking his head; just because three strangers had somehow destroyed the tightly woven net of deceit that had so nicely carried him to another night, another story, without ever asking him to show himself to anyone, let alone to himself.

Were they at least suffering the same way he was?

Were they at least in this too?

In front of Jonathan, five shirts were surrounding one perfumed trophy, because she was the only prey available, but Jonathan's nostrils were still filled with a very different scent, not really seductive, but somehow cushy, tender and sweet:

Was this it?

Was this the unfamiliar scent of an inside Jonathan had never wanted to hear anything about?

Damn it, this was still the jungle!

This was still the stray dog's home and there was no need to suddenly think through things that didn't need thinking through.

Jonathan pushed.

"Fuck," he said.

Jonathan reached down to his pocket and took out his mobile phone; all he wanted was a kiss, wasn't it? All he wanted was his lips touching someone else's; someone else's tongue touching his, and then everything would be good again. That was the only problem, wasn't it?

He looked at the mobile.

Whatever.

He pressed L just as a shadow entered his corner and whispered in a familiar voice:

"Pills?"

Sarah rubbed her arms, but it didn't help. She raised her head, but the cold water just bounced off her shivery body. This shower was as useless as the first one had been, hours ago: Sarah wasn't waking up.

Because this wasn't a dream.

"Are you mad?"

The sentence replayed in her head, again and again, her parents and Peter turning into one deafening shout.

"Are you completely out of your mind?"

The words came back at her as a terrible cacophony of disbelief and anger, a bright professional future ripped into pieces by her own hands:

A shooting spree of irrationality.

"Are you crazy, Sarah?"

She rubbed her face, but the painful picture they had thrown at her earlier didn't leave, thousands being kicked onto the streets of this city without a reason, a chance or mercy. There it was, all of sudden, the shocking reality that hadn't made it past Sarah's soothing veil in the past few days, thousands being dumped without any hope to ever be allowed in again.

And Sarah.

Handing herself over voluntarily.

She shuddered.

There it was, all of sudden, a situation so brutal and real it simply couldn't have been countered with her timid:

"But..."

How could she even have started to explain something that couldn't be explained to anyone who hadn't been there from the beginning?

"But..."

How could she even have tried?

Today, she had let everyone down; there was no talking round that anymore.

"Who's there?"

Sarah ripped away the shower curtain. She listened into the silence.

"Hello?"

But there was no one.

She let her hand sink again. Peter was miles away, his mobile switched off in protest. He had ended a terrible phone call in the cruellest way possible, his usual kindness replaced by an accusing bark.

"Talk soon, okay?" Sarah had whispered in the most demure voice she had ever heard herself speak in.

But Peter hadn't answered.

Peter had simply hung up, a reunion unconfirmed. Forgiveness unlikely?

Sarah shuddered.

Peter had never hung up on her before.

Peter had always ended their conversations with words Sarah had long come to take for granted, reassurance in every syllable, warmth in every word:

A stability Sarah hadn't even noticed?

She turned the water even colder.

But it didn't help.

This morning, she had thrown away the life Peter was determined to live with words no one would ever be able to edit out again:

"My decision is final. I'm going to leave, right now."

What.

Had.

She.

Done?

Sarah covered her ears, but the harder she tried to silence the torment, the louder it became.

Sarah turned off the water.

She didn't move.

The harder she tried to shut everyone up, the more terrified she grew of being left behind. Goosebumps started spreading all over her freezing body.

But she didn't move.

Why had even the one that had spoon-fed her the outside, until the tickling had turned into a conviction that had left her no other choice, fallen silent now?

Sarah rubbed her arms.

Why had even the one who was to blame for all this switched off his sympathy now?

"The person you are calling is not available at present."

Max had switched off his understanding.

"Please try again later," the voice had said, as Sarah had tried to return the calls she had missed, again and again:

"Please try again later."

Max had shut down his support for a deed that had been meant to bring Sarah thundering applause from all sides, her life taken into her own hands, finally, but left her alone with the opposite:

Choirs of contempt.

What.

Had.

She.

Done?

She stepped out of the shower cabin and took a step towards the small bathroom mirror, but the ghost didn't look back at her. The last remaining hint of confidence had gone the way her make-up had, revealing skin so naked and sensitive it threatened to fall apart at the slightest touch; she grabbed the biggest towel she could find and wrapped herself up in it.

But it didn't help.

Whatever it was, it could come closer:

She had never felt this vulnerable.

Ever.

Whatever it was, it could touch her and grab her throat and shake her and there was nothing she could do.

Sarah didn't move.

All life was being sucked away by a force she couldn't point at and all that prevented her from collapsing straight away was a vague feeling that it wasn't just her, slipping for the sake of something she couldn't point at either, but that idea was far too vague and distant and meaningless to prevent her from sinking, slowly:

Her deed couldn't be reversed.

Sarah wriggled.

Her deed wouldn't be forgiven and this terrible voice didn't stop.

She grabbed the sink for support, but the weight of shame and guilt that had been placed on her weak shoulders from somewhere pushed her down further.

Her deed wouldn't be forgiven:

She had destroyed her life.

She closed her eyes.

The regret that had come from nowhere only to take over her whole body pushed her down and all the way to the neatly tiled, cold white floor of her bathroom where this, suddenly, was between Sarah and Sarah:

There was no one left to hold her.

She trembled.

There was no one left to protect her, because Sarah herself had eliminated those that were meant to protect her with a smug shrug, their uniformed bodies drenched in a dreadful pool of blood...

She folded.

There was no one left to stop what was about to happen on the neatly tiled, cold white floor of her bathroom, but Sarah.

Lizzie couldn't help it.

She had to turn her head as she walked past the restaurant's window and look inside, where other people occupied the same table the four of them had occupied last night, too close to be true.

Too close to be real?

Lizzie turned away.

It didn't help being reminded how much she wanted to be like Sarah right now, or even like Max, and it didn't help at all being reminded how much she wanted to be with Jonathan, who still hadn't said a single word.

She crossed Shacklewell Lane at red.

No one had.

Lizzie tripped over a hundred Whisky Cokes.

"Fuck."

Back at The Marquis of Lansdowne, it had all been fine, for a few hours.

Back at The Marquis of Lansdowne, it had been okay, not having a job or a purpose or anything to cling to, but another cold and solid glass of oblivion, because her life still missed the foundations most people her age had long created for themselves.

For a few hours, it had been just fine.

She looked down.

Back at The Marquis of Lansdowne, where she had come for comfort the moment her bed had stopped providing it, no one had raised an eyebrow at Lizzie drowning her brain in booze, because she was still stuck between a hundred thousand options and no guidance, because life was like that:

You fucking chose.

And, unfortunately, everyone had long dumped a past, parents and whoever was sitting on that fluffy white cloud up there:

For a life-time wasted slithering.

Unfortunately, everyone had long branded every convention outmoded and all assistance fake and any kind of advice old-fashioned:

For a life-time, giving up this for that.

Ha!

For a life-time flip-flopping their shivery selves into an early grave, still proudly shouting, from the bottom of their tarnished souls, the supposedly liberated song that went by the name of freedom.

Freedom.

Freedom.

"But you know what?" Lizzie shouted at the pavement, and:

"You know what?"

She punched the air.

She shouted:

"Fuck freedom."

She tripped over her own feet; what was wrong with rules, for Christ's sake?

She caught herself.

What was ever wrong with a limit?

"Fuck it."

A bunch of drunken Dalstonites, all mad hairdos and neon trousers and high-pitch shrieks of joy, looked at her as if she was some kind of alien, all of a sudden, when all she wanted was someone to take away all the choice she had and tell her what to do and where to be and what to wear and what to say what the hell this was all about.

"Fuck it."

This life was still ruled by question marks and all she needed was a hand, grabbing hers.

All she wanted was being led.

But Jonathan hadn't uttered a single fucking word since yesterday.

And that was worst of all.

Lizzie let her hand glide along the cold metal shutters that covered the junk jewellery and the cheap cosmetics and the dried butcher blood. All the shops were closed by now, the whole stretch dead.

Clack.

Clack.

Clack.

It seemed as if Lizzie was damned to stay on the outside, just as the inside she had resisted all her life was appearing more tempting than it ever had.

Clack.

Clack.

Clack.

She turned the corner and was greeted by the biting smell of piss and rot that covered the market once the worst rubbish had been swept away for the day. The Christmas lights had been switched off a long time ago. At this time, Ridley Road was nothing but a creepy, forsaken side street, where the rats were coming out.

"Pound a bowl," Lizzie screamed into the darkness.

"Pound a bowl."

How she had loved this market once.

How she had adored this, the great swallow-up, where a hundred voices united to become one defiant roar against the real world, golden-toothed lunatics next to humpbacked grannies mumbling to a pavement covered in tomatoes and cardboard mush and yet another would-be beauty queen for a contest that would still have to be invented.

"Comeandhavealook!"

How she had needed this wonderful place once, determined to soak up all of its mad energy and turn it into art that wasn't just good, but great.

How inspired she had been, once.

Lizzie fumbled for her keys.

For today, the stalls had been pushed away, but everything would start again tomorrow, wouldn't it?

There was always another day.

Lizzie searched for the lock.

There was always another week.

Lizzie turned the key and pushed the door. There was always another chance, wasn't there?

She grabbed for hold that wasn't there.

She tripped.

She fell, a thousand shoes sending her Whisky-heated face crashing against the filthy carpet that covered the stairs and that was that.

"Hurray," she mumbled, and:

"Hurray."

She closed her eyes and started breathing dust, fully determined to stay exactly where she was, just as a voice said from behind:

"Lizzie?"

A dream.

A vision.

A lie.

"You alright?"

Lizzie tried to open her eyes.

What a fucked-up fancy, being picked up from behind, two strong arms beneath her armpits.

Getting saved.

What a mad dream, looking into eyes sparkling in a kind of blue that was hard to ignore.

"I tried to call, but..."

A piece of fiction, flinging her weak arms around his neck, dazed and confused, holding on.

And on.

And on.

The wishful thinking of a drunk, being caught only to land in a pair of arms she had tried to forget all day, mindlessly allowing his lips to find hers, finally, blurry-eyed standing in the doorway of her flat, surrounded by a thousand shoes, kissing and being kissed and on.

And on.

And on.

A flimsy illusion, being led up the stairs, step for step for step, keeping her resistance where it was best kept to enjoy

being taken, through the door of her flat and into her room, where the crushed cans of Stella formed a sculpture to mark the life of Lizzie, the artist, and being dragged onto her mattress and letting go, finally, for the day's final hallucination, stripping away her black top and pulling up his tight shirt and having her bra ripped down and feeling a touch, suddenly, that left no doubt whether this was real, or not.

Max stumbled on.

For what seemed hours, he had been passing closed metal gates, abandoned cars and Victorian houses that wouldn't be visible if it wasn't for their white satellite dishes. Every street had started to look like the previous one, Hackney's trademark diversity destroyed by darkness and his daze...

Where the hell was he?

Max stopped.

Why the hell was this still dragging on?

The wreck of a former pub that rose next to him was about to collapse, just like everything had. Foul wooden boards were holding together the crumbling red stone. Ashes covered the pavement. The decade's rumble was all around him, broken clock hands buried in the dust of despair:

Nothing was ticking anymore.

On this forsaken street, as everywhere else, the failure was evident on every corner:

A whole generation was watching this terrible fall with its collective arms crossed, casually.

As if by default.

As if by default, eyes had been closed and ears had been shut and that was that...

Max looked up.

In front of him, two bare electricity masts rose into the sky and the flashback was inevitable, the memory far too fresh, looking down from atop Springfield's hill, where he had seen exactly what would spread behind those trees.

Where all restraint had been left behind in favour of words that had felt like a long and dreamy kiss. Another moment Max would never be able to forget.

He looked down again.

Was this really where his confused walk from The Elderfield had led him?

The creepy power station at the mast's bottom gave way to a small concrete bridge.

Was this it?

It was all still far too present, wrong signals, leading to wrong assumptions, leading to an ill-fated attempt on a Stoke Newington couch that had killed the sweet promise Mangal had made.

"See you soon, okay?" she had said on her doorstep.

But Sarah was gone.

Having rubbed everything Max would never have into his critical wounds, Sarah had left him behind.

"See you soon. And – I'm sorry again."

"Don't worry," she had said on her doorstep, but couldn't have meant any of it.

Otherwise she would be here with him now.

Max left behind the last remaining houses and the last remaining cars and walked towards the small bridge in front of him. Only a row of lifeless, looming willows separated him from the marshes now. He let his hands glide over the coarse, cold concrete as he stepped onto the bridge. Down there, the river Lee was a motionless black something that didn't have to think twice about joining this terrible sneer.

He shouldn't have survived.

He should have died in the trenches, in a pool of blood, for everyone to see:

A name on a cross.

A wake-up call.

A martyr for a cause no one had taken up yet, cosy living rooms like bomb shelters and a remote to switch it all away: on other channels, happier stories.

But he had.

In the distance, a lonely red cone stuck out of the muddy water like a shark fin.

Just because the medicine that had been administered, from the cradle onwards and in doses higher than anyone could have found healthy, had turned sour on them, all of a sudden.

Max walked on.

Just because a supposedly God-given truth called capitalism had been debunked in front of everyone's eyes for those that had never known anything but to bear the brunt; Max walked beneath the willows and there it was.

He stopped.

There it was, stretching in front of him without a warning; he looked left and he looked right, but it was already spreading all around him:

Nothing.

There it was, finally, right into his face; Max took a few careful steps on the half-frozen, lifeless ground. In the far distance, a row of bare trees lined the sky, almost too vague to see. A few football goals scattered the marshes like loners, but apart from that:

Nothing.

Max turned around, but it was too late: it was moving in on him, finally.

Max looked left again and Max looked right, but it was too late:

He was surrounded.

He had no choice, but to give in.

Nothing pushed Max down and he landed on his knees. He had no choice, but to do what he had tried to avoid for years now, semi-proud struggling on in a vain hope that things would work out eventually, and that was the flag, finally.

That was surrender.

Here it was, his ultimate acknowledgement, never to have done anything in his life, but to wait.

Never to have done anything but to sit surrounded by what other people had thought and had sharpened and had published and damn all that; not to have achieved a single thing in his life, but this shameful scene, weak arms folding in a defeat that was not to be watched by anyone, as the bitter truth started entering his veins:

He would never make this world a better place.

His head started sinking:

The battle was lost.

The dream was dead and there was no other dream left and he would never do any of the things he had romanticised for hours and hours in front of Sarah's glowing eyes, because the world was writing a different story now and there was nothing Max could do about it, was there?

A few pebbles bored into his forehead as he reached the ground.

Max simply caved in.

He was no longer willing to wait for anything.

He closed his eyes.

He was no longer willing to suffer from all those beautiful moments spent with someone he would never be able to impress with anything again.

The last remaining strength left his body.

He simply accepted.

His muscles started loosening and there, in the middle of the deserted marshes, finally, a single tear started running down his right cheek and dropped onto the frozen, lifeless ground without a sound...

For just a moment, it seemed as if someone wanted to say something to Max, but the voice wasn't getting through. Instead, the nothingness that surrounded him started covering his shivering body like a large and heavy blanket.

Ejaculate and run?

Lizzie hastened down a forsaken Kingsland High Street where it became a forsaken Kingsland Road; she couldn't believe Jonathan had left her like that, rushing up the moment they had finished, two warm bodies pressed against each other, his warm breath against her neck for just a moment...

"I need to go."

"What?"

"I..."

Pants.

Socks.

Jeans.

"Where do you need to go in the middle of night?"

"I..."

"What?"

T-shirt.

Coat.

Shoes.

"Thanks."

"Thanks?"

"I'm sorry."

"What's wrong with you?"

She couldn't believe he had left her like that, out of her door and down the creaky stairs and gone, taking the soothing smell of sex and warmth and affection, leaving Lizzie, naked, cold and done.

"What the hell?"

She still couldn't believe she was rushing after him like that, tumbling through the streets of Hackney without any idea where he might be.

"Arsehole," she screamed.

Her lipstick was all over the place. She was wearing her t-shirt the wrong way round.

How the hell could he treat her like that, running away to rub his insatiable dick against some other girl's arse in a Dalston basement as if nothing had happened?

Not the greedy kissing.

Not the tender touch, without either of them having to say a word.

Not this wonderful closeness.

Lizzie sobbed.

"What the hell," she said and kicked the air in front of her. She had no idea if the alcohol that had nearly knocked her out earlier was gone or not. Everything around her was one muddle, the blue sirens and the neon minaret and the night bus that was just swishing past without any regard.

Lizzie stopped.

She pinched her eyes; this was it, three words like a knife and now this, a final stab.

This was the canal, wasn't it?

Lizzie leaned against the black metal railing that lined Kingsland Road where it crossed the Regent's Canal on its way to Islington. In the shiny new flats on the right and the remodelled waterside warehouse on the left, almost all lights had been switched off.

Those with normal lives had gone to bed.

Lizzie took out her mobile.

How could she have allowed herself to be pushed like that, from Catch to the Russian to wherever, as if all this had been some kind of beginning, for a change, and all the way here, no longer able to explain herself to anyone and not even able to explain herself to herself anymore.

Lizzie clutched the mobile.

How could she have allowed herself to be lifted like that only to be dropped with no choice but to run into the arms of her parents and admit, once and for all, what she didn't want to admit?

Lizzie leaned forward.

Down there, the canal was as black as the sky would be, if it wasn't for this city turning it orange night after night.

She sighed.

This city.

The great hope.

Which had invited her as it had invited many, its seducing arms stretched from Victoria Park's lawns to Notting Hill, welcoming every tongue and fetish, belief or root: to fulfil their potential and grab the opportunities with both hands.

This city.

The great promise.

Which had invited her as it had invited many to become whatever they had wanted to become.

Lizzie swallowed.

And then hadn't let them.

Exit, the flip.

Exit, the flop.

Exit, the defeated, told and forgotten; she clutched. The promise was broken.

The dream was dead.

And that meant that the curtain could fall, if only this was a play, thundering applause and white wine from the bar as the cleaners brushed away whatever was left of whatever had happened, but unfortunately this wasn't a play.

Unfortunately, this was real life.

And that was irritating, but it wasn't really her fault that this world had swallowed her humour and her drive and her liveliness and all those things that had made her such a lovely person to spend time with, once, was it?

It all wasn't really her fault, was it?

Lizzie pressed herself harder against the railing in front of her, not to slide down further.

Was she really resisting this?

She pressed.

Was she really putting up a fight, now, finally?

Lizzie placed the phone onto the narrow railing, where it lay in a delicate balance.

Whatever warmth and comfort had overcome her inside Mangal, was being replaced by the most terrible sense of abandonment she had ever felt and, standing on this god-forsaken bridge in the middle of this god-forsaken night in her god-forsaken city there was suddenly no doubt about it at all anymore:

Not today and not tomorrow.

Not on nicely set family dining tables, where the lie had been spread, and not on shabby flatshare ones, where they had believed in it.

Not in this city and not in any other city.

Not today.

And not tomorrow; Lizzie rose to her tiptoes. Her pumping veins rubbed over the cold metal.

Wasn't it totally obvious?

Lizzie pushed, left, right.

Nothing was possible anymore.

And nothing would ever be possible again, all her chances squandered, and now, there was only one choice left, because life was like that:

You chose.

To live.

Or to die, absolute freedom's glorious peak; the mobile dropped.

There was a numb splash and then there was silence, as Lizzie clasped the only thing that was left to clasp, cold metal against her tummy and tiptoe trembled in a silent cry, swaying on and on and on...

"Shit," Jonathan said; he had fucking fucked Lizzie exactly the way he had fucking fucked all the others, hadn't he?

"Shit, shit, shit."

He had mindlessly used her, until his orgasm had kick-started these lines like machine gun fire, and the ripples were still flowing through his body:

Lizzie was so much more than he had admitted to her, wasn't she?

"Shit."

Lizzie was so much more than he had admitted to himself.

"Shit, shit, shit."

And how on earth could he have avoided leaving her the way he had?

A condom filled with shame.

A body filled with disgust.

A mind in a blurry new terrain he hadn't even known existed; how on earth could he have acted any differently, as he had received that hammer blow to his drug-damaged head?

Fuck.

He had abused the only person in this world that mattered.

Jonathan looked up.

The dirty brown light bulb that was hanging from the crumbling ceiling would die any minute now. The air around him smelled fouler by the minute, but Jonathan was still alive, wasn't he?

He leaned against the wall.

He was still breathing.

"Hell-o?" he screamed, but there was no reply, only this relentless drip, drip, drip:

In the corner, the puddle was growing.

His shoes stuck to the sludge that covered the whole floor of this so-called venue off Kingsland High Street.

"Heee-looo!"

Even though venue was hardly the right word.

"Anyone?"

And he should have known the moment they had told him it was called The Bunker.

"Heee-looo!"

But there was no answer. Everyone had gone; The Bunker was deserted.

"Anyone?"

The horn-rimmed would-bes that had flyer-lured him through the dark walkway and down the narrow stairs and here had left him with their so-called creative output and now the dripping didn't stop.

Jonathan kicked the metal something in front of him.

The level was rising.

He swung around and banged his fist against the moist wall behind him, but the lump that had started to seize his stomach the moment he had come inside Lizzie wasn't going away, despite the can of Carlsberg he had downed the moment he had entered this underground labyrinth in search of a fix, fully aware that this couldn't be fixed with a can of Carlsberg, or a line or two, or any of those tricks that had so nicely carried him until three strangers had re-introduced responsibility and consequence.

Fuck.

Jonathan didn't move.

It was as if realisation itself was dripping from the crumbling ceiling above him.

Drip.

There was no way he could continue to hold up his individualism in order to hide what could no longer be hidden, was there?

Using himself as an excuse.

Drip.

There was no way he could just continue to stride through the bars of his city pretending whatever was required, while all he desired fell straight into his lap without him having to raise a finger, was there?

Drip.

Fighting alone, but for what?

Drip.

The city that had always been just like him, all sorts of things to all sorts of people, was finally handing him what it had always pretended would not exist.

Drip.

Drip.

Drip.

Jonathan banged his fist against the wall; this orgasm had ripped something out of him he hadn't even known existed, only to fill every pore of his body with whatever had started in the Russian Bar or inside Mangal or wherever it had started and it wasn't going away.

Jonathan banged the wall again, but he didn't feel anything.

Where was she now?

And where was Sarah and what was Max up to and why did he even care, suddenly?

Jonathan punched himself, fist against his chest, but that didn't do anything either.

Were they with him now?

He punched again.

Did they still feel what he couldn't?

There was no tickling in his lungs and there was no bubbling in his veins and there was no reaction from any part of his body to anything at all anymore.

There was only this lump.

But that wasn't a physical problem; Jonathan banged his head against the wall.

As if steered?

He had arrived where he had arrived, but this fucked-up mind was unable to make the next step.

He banged again and more forcefully this time.

The way out was hidden; honesty and commitment were performing their slow dance somewhere far away from here, behind closed doors, out of reach.

He banged harder.

The way up was still closed.

And harder.

And harder.

Jonathan didn't stop the flow as it finally happened, a thick red trickle towards feeling something, anything, and the clattering that streamed at him from all sides left no doubt.

This was it.

This was still the only answer he had; the deafening drone that took over his body from his head downwards could only mean one thing. This relentless thudding had only one explanation, and that was still all he could come up with in response to this or anything...

Jonathan slithered into the sludge.

Max jumped up.

As if resurrected, he rose from the lifeless, frozen ground of the marshes.

Everything turned.

As if another force was lifting him up, finally, and Max began to smile.

He wanted to slap himself.

He whirled around.

He wanted to slap himself, again and again, for not having realised much earlier what had just hit him so hard he wanted to scream:

The bombs were hitting other places.

He wanted to slap them too, all three of them, wherever they were just pitying themselves to the ground, because things weren't quite working out, out-moaning each about their supposedly miserable lives inside Mangal, without any idea what they had been talking about:

The rockets were killing other children.

Max wanted to yell.

The real blood was flowing elsewhere, but he had never been forced to be there.

And neither had any of them.

Those that had every reason to use the word miserable in connection with their lives were getting on with it, but Max had never been forced to see any of it, because, around here, the air-raid sirens had stopped wailing a long time ago.

Could they hear him?

Max wanted to bang all four of their heads together, again and again, for the pathetic show they had staged in the last few days, sinking to the ground just because, for once in their life, this world was refusing to give them what they had come to expect from birth onwards:

Everything.

And all at once.

And immediately; Max started shaking his head. Just because their relentless quest for total satisfaction had taken its first ever hit and wasn't, for a change, handing them the absolute self-fulfilment they had grown up feeling entitled to.

Max wanted to slap and hug them at the same time.

He took a deep breath.

How clear it seemed, all of sudden; exhaling, his breath became a small white plume in the cold night-time air. Around him, there was still only darkness. The sprawling marshes kept away the light that governed London everywhere else:

The sky was almost black.

Max looked up again.

The moment that had just passed would stay with him forever, slowly opening his eyes, his cold and stiff arms next to a motionless body, only to see more stars than he had ever seen in this city and the result was still flowing through his veins, an existence so small and meaningless, yet part of something so much bigger.

Max started smiling.

So alive.

Max wanted to dance with himself.

So very alive.

Max wanted to know where it was coming from, suddenly, a life that wasn't going quite as expected, but was still the most precious thing any of them would ever have, and a world that might be a little fucked up, but would never stop being the most extraordinary thing any of them would ever experience.

He whirled around.

Like a beautiful ballerina that had finally discovered her rhythm, he turned round and round:

Could they see him?

This was unbelievable, a voice whispering from somewhere, anywhere, nowhere, that everything that had collapsed had to be built again.

That everything could be built differently.

His mouth opened.

Everything could be built so much better, couldn't it?

His eyes grew.

The big crash that, only a few hours ago, had seemed to finish everything was only the beginning, wasn't it?

His chin dropped.

This, right here, right now, was the beginning of a whole new era, wasn't it?

These thoughts electrified Max in a way nothing had ever electrified him before.

This, right here, was it.

He wiped away the sweat from his forehead and started walking, head raised, like a dazed wanderer that had finally found his way:

This was a whole new world now and who was to shape it, if not them?

Max wanted to explode.

This was the chance of a lifetime.

He took out his phone.

There was still so much energy and there was still so much time; there was so much to do and they only had to start doing it and the rest would simply become clear as they went along, wouldn't it?

He switched on his phone.

They only had to come together in a way they had never done before and kick off something no one had ever kicked off; Max punched the air.

His mobile announced a flurry of text messages he had missed since he had left The Elderfield hours ago...

He ducked below the willows.

The lights of the first high rises announced the mixed-up madhouse he called home. There it was again, the place where the slow-burning excitement of non-belonging had over time turned into an alienation that had just been replaced by a completely new hope:

Max could already hear the shouts.

He could already feel the heat.

The picture was already clearer than any picture had ever been.

All he had to do was to find a way to be heard...

He looked at his mobile.

"Call me immediately," the text said, and:

"Something terrible has happened."

Four months later

Pearls of sweat ran down their foreheads as they closed ranks in a way none of them had thought possible, shoulder against shoulder towards the only outcome this fired-up crowd was willing to accept; it was all happening:

They pushed on.

It was all clear:

From face to face, sparkling with an unseen determination and from eye to eye, glowing with a mad new drive, everyone in this fired-up crowd knew perfectly well that they had nothing to lose on these streets, but a future to win.

And there was no return.

For the first time in their lives they were joining hands and turning around was no longer an option.

Everyone knew that, too.

Everyone understood that too much had happened for that already.

Street after street, the fight-back was on and you had to be blind not to see that they were coming closer by the day:

"Together!"

Push by push, they were getting stronger.

"Everyone!"

Step by step, everyone got a little more determined to go all the way, a thousand raging shouts ringing through the streets of central London, because they had to. Because the pictures weren't going away:

Barren landscapes.

Flooded cities.

Guns being handed over to those that were left. To fight for whatever else was.

"Onwards!"

Street after street, instructions weren't needed, because the message on everyone's lips wasn't prescribed, for a change, but came straight from the heart:

Those that had been pushed to the ground had risen.

Those December had threatened to take were emerging, stronger than they had ever felt in their lives and these scenes were more beautiful than anything anyone had ever seen, a thousand fists raised towards an April sun in a final go at grabbing this away from those that had abused their power for far too long now.

These scenes were taking everyone's breath away.

Street after street, this was on.

Street after street, this was happening just the way he had imagined it.

And there was only one reason the masses were rising up the way they did, out there, and that reason was being streamed out from a small table in the corner of a warehouse-turned-café in a Dalston side street, where another sentence was just being trimmed for maximum effect:

"All we need is you."

Where excitement was beating the doubt, once again.

Because there was only one reason things were kicking off the way they were and that reason was him.

Max rushed up.

There was no doubt about it:

They were nearly there.

The vision that drove him out of bed a little earlier by the day was becoming a reality and sticking together the way everyone was, all of a sudden, no one could stop them.

That was the beauty of it.

He sat down again.

Realising all this was better than any drug in the world could ever be.

But he had to stay calm.

He leaned back; around him, a few early risers were looking at their screens, turning pages, sipping froth. Café Oto, the industrial-look, music-minded café he had chosen for this unorthodox operation, was filling up slowly. In the background, Dylan was tangled up in blue; across the bare, low-ceilinged room from Max, horn-rimmed students were ordering the homemade cookies and strong coffees that were his only consumption on the way from a blank new page to another perfectly composed post.

Ready to convince those that remained to be convinced.

Max looked at his screen.

Ready to push forward a mission that would change the world forever.

Max deleted the only paragraph he had written so far, without reading it again and opened the small black notebook that was filled with loose thoughts: broken fragments, scribbled while walking the streets of Hackney, to be used, processed, discarded. He needed another threat, a new angle.

He needed more punch.

He turned the page:

"Cells of discontent."

Line for line, it was being revived in here.

"Cells of rage."

Line for line, it came back:

Long lost phrases collided with half-forgotten words as another paperless pamphlet came together in the secrecy of night.

Finally, Max had an outlet.

Finally, Max had a way to say all he had to say, filling another blog post with a whole new meaning, so it could become what it had to become.

Finally, there was an audience.

And it was growing by the hour...

And soon they would have convinced all those that still believed the hollow words uttered by those that continued to smile into the cameras as if nothing had happened.

"They had their chance."

His fingers hovered.

"And they squandered it."

His finger flew across the keyboard.

"But now, WE are winning."

Max shouted at his screen:

"Because everyone is coming together!"

The couple that ran Café Oto glanced at him from behind their counter, but they had long started tolerating his eruptions, the rushing up and down, the screams of joy when a sentence was coming together, finally.

He nodded at them.

"Because..."

He leaned back.

On the other side of the window that stretched from the floor to the ceiling next to him, the diggers were eating away at Dalston's fabric. Chunk for chunk, the past was being eradicated for a train network this borough had so nicely managed without until now. The dull thudding of the pneumatic hammers joined the usual medley of sirens and honks for a tune that had the power to take Max way from this, thousands still to be convinced.

His eyes lost focus.

This was the serenading song that could silence the worries about this world's future.

Only to invite the past again?

Max sighed.

Who was he kidding?

Who was he trying to fool by pretending that their delirious December ride, seem from here, an April sun hinting at something that could be called spring, had become some meaningless back story, filed and forgotten?

What was the point trying to forget his feverish run from the half-frozen ground of the marshes, his mobile still in his hand, to attend a scene that just wouldn't leave his head?

Four pale faces, just like one.

Four strangers, reunited, only that, this time, no one had laughed.

Only that, this time, no one had quite known what to say, blinded by fluorescent lights that had only multiplied the shock they had felt, looking at each other in a shameful silence.

As if what had come to him in the marshes hadn't been enough.

Max let his fingers glide down.

As if another force had tried to underline it all by taking him where they treated those suffering from ailments slightly more serious than confusion.

Max rushed away from the window.

There was no time for this.

Everything that was happening was happening because of that night in December, but in less than an hour he had to be ready. He pulled himself closer to the table again. What had happened in the fluorescent light had bonded the four of them together in a way none of them could have expected,

Mangal having been a mere foretaste, but there was no space for this now; Max placed his fingers on the keyboard and tried to concentrate again. He had to get this post into shape if he wanted her smile in admiration to finally turn into more today.

The burnt plastic stuck to her Converse as Lizzie stepped through the wreckage that dominated this, the zone: large piles of debris gave way to cut wires, tyres, mush; a rusty old canister rocked in the wind. Lizzie carefully balanced over the remains of a plastic window frame; she was still shivery.

She was still here.

The wind blew gusts of ashes over the shattered glass; in front of her, the remains of a swivel chair crumbled in-between burst bags of whatever had seemed important before December had torn everything into pieces.

Lizzie smiled.

She was picking them up.

That was all that mattered.

She stepped over a rotten pallet and onto the pavement, where the graffiti-covered blue gates led her to the disintegrating door of her studio; she was using whatever had survived the final word and the result was getting better with every day she spent inside here.

Lizzie took two stairs at the time.

The smell of piss that filled the cold and empty corridor was no less disgusting than three weeks ago, when an unsure face had finally given in to signs that couldn't have been any clearer:

This was the perfect place.

This was the perfect time.

This was it, finally; on the third floor, the white wooden door stood open the way she had left it, since locking anything in this ghost house would be a joke:

This was Hackney Wick, after all.

This was the edge.

Lizzie let the pack of Golden Virginia drop onto the cotton bag that was lying on the concrete floor and looked at her piece, rising majestically in the middle of her room.

"Here we go..."

Surrounded by chimneys that had stopped emitting anything and gates that protected nothing, Lizzie was finally able to hear a voice that had been muted for far too long.

Surrounded by poison, dust and sewage, Lizzie could finally listen to herself.

She looked up and down her piece.

Everything that had built up inside of her in the last few months was flowing into this structure.

She took a step towards it.

And seeing it all come together like that was almost enough to make her forget what it had taken to get to this point.

Lizzie reached out to touch it.

Was that her phone?

She turned around and bent down to get the mobile out of her cotton bag and looked at the display and said:

"Fuck."

She had forgotten about this completely, arranged three weeks in advance, probably in a vain hope that Claire would too. Which, of course, she hadn't.

"Fuck," Lizzie said, picked up and said:

"Hey, honey."

The first catch-up since the last catch-up had pushed the first domino, a bottle of white wine in-between them.

"Hey Lizzie, still up for tonight?"

But Claire had no idea what had happened afterwards, because, until now, she hadn't followed up her casual remark, a bait without consideration.

"Yes, sure," Lizzie said.

Claire hadn't seen the Russian or The George or anything at all and there was no way Lizzie would re-heat what had cooled down so nicely.

"Seven still good?"

It was always seven, but at least Lizzie had convinced Claire to meet in Dalston this time.

"Yep."

She would get a white-washed take, there was no question about it.

"Cool."

Lizzie would simply tell this story the way it would look in a few months' time, from a wiser position: a straight walk, from the Oak to the Wick.

"Okay, see you later," Lizzie said.

And in that particular film, there were no scenes on bridges.

Lizzie pressed red.

She had no time for this.

In front of her door, the bulldozers droned a little louder by the day. The wrecking ball could hit any minute and no one knew who would survive, and who wouldn't, just like out there, in the real world, where the getting through was unconfirmed, the struggle still on.

Lizzie walked over to the window and opened it.

Out there, the April sun tried, but failed, to break through clouds that were refusing to go away.

Bits of paint came off as Lizzie leaned against the window sill.

She took a deep breath.

The dust tickled her nose, but she was used to that by now. The air wasn't exactly healthy around here, but the state of her lungs didn't matter.

All that mattered was rising in the middle of this bare room.

All that mattered was Lizzie.

But tonight Claire would ask the questions Claire was born to ask and Lizzie would have to work hard to steer around a night that had ended with four pale faces on Ward Two.

Lizzie turned away hastily.

She would never forget how Max had finally broken the silence with a speech that had sounded as pompous as everything he had ever said, but, unfortunately, his tone hadn't cancelled out the truth in every word he had sent through the room and right into their ears:

"It all came to me in the marshes."

How surreal it all sounded...

Heard from here, several big steps on from realisations that had started that very moment.

"Isn't that mad?" Max had said, and:

"I mean, what a wake-up call!"

And Lizzie had nodded without saying anything, as a new road had started appearing in front of her.

How distant it all seemed...

Seen from here, several big steps on from the careful smile she had carefully accepted as she had looked away from Max and into a pair of eyes that had looked warmer and more caring than they had ever before; Lizzie took a few steps towards her piece and sighed.

"What is it?" Jonathan said, but colleague Natalie just stared at him.

"What?"

She was already playing the role he was about to play for the next eight hours, pretending what had to be pretended until this office would release him again, down the stairs and up the road, towards a place called home and a bed that was harder to leave than any bed had ever been.

Everything was fluid.

That much was clear.

"There's a note for you," Natalie said.

"What do you mean, note?"

Jonathan looked at his desk, where the crumpled, greasy brown bags from the bagel shop piled next to the encrusted coffee cups from the café across the road. It was written on the backside of a used A4 sheet that was folded in half.

Natalie turned away.

"Right," Jonathan said.

"You'd better hurry."

He walked past Natalie towards the only closed door in their open plan office.

"Don't you worry."

What was that all about, his presence requested before he even had a chance to switch on his machine?

Jonathan knocked and entered without waiting.

"Morning," he said.

"Morning."

"What's up?" he said.

"Why don't you sit down?" he heard and did and looked into an expression more serious than anything he had ever seen on this particular face, a boss like a mate, Friday night pints and a shared cigarette, but not this:

"There isn't a nice way of saying this, Jonathan."

"Saying what?"

"We have to make you redundant, it's a terrible situation, but we have no choice. I'm very sorry."

He looked at Jonathan and Jonathan looked at him, but the words were still trying to force their way past the smell of sex that hadn't left his nose all the way here, and the anticipation of another shared bottle of wine on their small balcony.

"Redundant," he said, unsure if there was a question mark in his pronunciation, or not.

"Times are tough, Jonathan. For all of us. As I said, I'm terribly sorry. But there is no other way."

The words were still only breaking through this newly erected wall of happiness.

Jonathan just nodded.

"Redundant," he said again, but then the meaning arrived and he burst out:

"So why me?"

A boss like a mate that had just turned into a pig, huffing and puffing.

"Don't you know this yourself, Jonathan?"

"No?"

"Your work is...well, it's okay, but not much more than that and in the current climate –"

"Brilliant."

"I thought I had given you signals, Jonathan. I think Natalie has given you signals as well. I told her to, anyway. But I guess, those never reached you?"

"Signals?"

Jesus.

"Look, Jonathan, this isn't the end of the world. We'll let you go with good references."

"As if anyone still cared for references."

Even Jonathan had followed enough news reports to know what was going on by now.

"I know it's tough out there, but –"

"But what?"

"Perhaps you should have thought about that before you started letting things slip the way you have. I mean, it's not that we never noticed..."

Jonathan just looked at him.

But everything was changing!

All was coming good, a new place, a new life. A few weeks, a few months: a whole new situation.

Wasn't that so clear to see?

Didn't this pig, huffing and puffing, understand anything at all?

"As I said, Jonathan, I'm terribly sorry, but I really don't see any other way right now. You can leave straight away or stay until the end of the month, it's up to you. I thought I'd give you that option."

"How very generous of you."

"Please, Jonathan, let's keep this civilised, okay?"

Civilised?

He was being sacked in the face of all his good intentions and this ladder-climbing monster was talking about keeping things civilised?

"What do you think?"

Jonathan rushed up.

"Do you really think I'd hang around this hell hole of an office any minute longer after this? Do you really think that? I couldn't think of anything worse than to stay to the end of the month."

He turned around.

"I'm off right now."

He left without closing the door, rushed to his desk and grabbed his bag.

"What's, hey, Jonathan..."

He ignored Natalie, pushed the chair towards his desk and walked over to the exit door.

"What's wrong, Jonathan?"

He pushed.

"What's wrong? As if you didn't know yourself. I'm leaving, that's what's wrong. I'm off."

"But it's only ten in the morning."

"Don't pretend to be stupid, Natalie. They're sacking me. They are generous enough to let me go."

"But –"

She got up, but Jonathan walked through the door and let it fall shut behind him, down the stairs and up the road and what? He ignored the reception girl in her mascara overkill and pushed the entrance door.

How on earth was he supposed not to fall back into the old pattern, Grolsch for breakfast?

A line for lunch.

He walked across the empty courtyard. Around the corner, Café 1001 would already be serving ice cube-cooled cans of Red Stripe to those that hadn't changed their lives as drastically as he had, after a night in December had shown him that his life was as fragile as everybody else's, despite his attempts to cover that unpleasant truth in a haze of booze.

That even Jonathan of the Shoreditch night sometimes encountered connections that couldn't just be cut:

"So, here we are."

They had all nodded, one like the other, after Max had delivered his silencing sermon, but his own shock had only started its fade the moment his weakly dangling hand had felt the careful touch of another, their shy fingers entangling until they had become a grip too firm and committed for anyone to break.

Neither then, in the fluorescent shine.

Nor now.

Jonathan turned around the corner.

Was that the deal?

If you were alright here, you couldn't be there? He had no savings; he had no plan. How on earth was he supposed to tell Lizzie?

He had no words; he had no idea.

Sarah closed the door behind her and walked straight to the makeshift-looking counter:

Retreat was not an option.

Having arrived where she had arrived, leaving this was out of the question.

"Can I have a cappuccino, please?"

This assurance was all she needed.

"Sure," he said and click-clacked the ground coffee into Sarah's nostrils, where it concluded the morning's usual procession, from kebab meat to flowers to fish to bagels to petrol to the self-rolled puffs of a Turkish grandfather on pavement patrol.

"How are you today?"

If you walked a street often enough, it became part of you and Sarah walked Stoke Newington High Street at least twice a day now.

"Very well, thanks."

She turned away from the machine's familiar huffing, towards the half-empty room, and smiled: there he was already, hammering away as if it was the last thing he would ever do on this earth.

She turned around.

"There you go. You're paying at the end of the day again?"

"Yes, thanks."

She grabbed the cup and walked towards the table in the corner, but he didn't look up:

This was another piece in the making and, right now, nothing else was getting in, or out.

"Good morning," she said, placed the cup on the table and sat down next to him.

His face was glued to the screen.

"Hey..." he mumbled.

His head was tuned to another frequency.

"Just a second."

"Sure," she said and turned away a little. She pulled her jumper over her head and started shaking her hair, made a ponytail and pulled up her lose black top a little, before turning around towards Max again.

He was already looking at her.

"So have you slept here again?" she said.

"Very funny."

"Wouldn't surprise me."

"I'm onto another cracker, Sarah."

His eyes were glowing.

"Just give me another few minutes, okay?"

She nodded, but Max was back already, typing as if someone else was directing him.

As if someone was pushing these words out of his brain and onto the page, out of his mind and into the world, where they would do exactly what they had to do. Sarah took out her laptop and opened the screen.

"So what's it on?"

"What?"

"The new post, what is it about?"

"Ahm," he said without looking at her.

"I see."

"I'm actually just changing my mind. I think I need a walk."

"You stuck?"

"No, no, it's just, you know..."

She nodded.

He was stuck, of course, but, as usual, unable to admit it. As usual, Max couldn't quite get himself to be honest with her, too scared to risk scarring the perfect image he was portraying of himself in here, every morning like another episode in a film that showed its protagonist in all his romantic, black and white glory:

The revival of a dying breed.

The return of the revolution's pen, when nothing was more badly needed than that.

"A few more days, Sarah," he said and leaned back.

"I can feel it so strongly. What's happening out there couldn't be any clearer."

She smiled.

"Soon we can go for the big one."

"Great," she said, as he got up, grabbed his jumper and walked towards the door. Sarah stretched to begin her part of the operation, but Max turned around again and looked at her.

"What?" she said.

"Ahm... Just wondering..."

He came towards her again.

"Just...are you doing anything tonight?"

She pressed the button to start her laptop and said, without looking at Max:

"I'm having dinner with Peter, yes."

"Okay, well I just thought, you know..."

"You know that it's not a good idea to have drinks during the week, don't you?"

He nodded.

"Yes, sorry, don't worry. See you in a bit, okay? I won't be long."

She smiled at him.

"Don't worry. Take your time, I'm not running away."

Because the running away had stopped.

The shying away had ended and so had the lying, to herself or to anyone.

"Oh and..."

Max leaned down and Sarah presented her cheeks, a ritual she accepted, first left, then right.

"I forgot earlier," he said and smiled the smile of a little child.

"I had already wondered," she said, and:

"Off you go."

Rambling the streets of Hackney to regain his flow, picking up ideas like the drifters picked up cigarette stubs. For Max, there seemed to be inspiration on every turn and it was hard to believe that he had ever managed to contain the energy that was flowing through his body.

Sarah watched him disappear towards Dalston Lane, before she peered onto his screen.

"For now, they are filming us..."

She smiled.

Post for post, Max was mobilising the masses in a way she had never thought possible, not even in her wildest dreams, writing himself into a frenzy that was incited by anger, but produced nothing but hope.

"For now they are registering us into yet another database, but they know this as much as we do."

She stretched to scroll down.

"That soon, there will be too many of us to be filmed. Look at them, shivering, because they know it all too well."

Post for post, Max was setting his words on fire in a way Sarah had never managed, not even in her best pieces.

"That soon there will be more of us than any database will hold."

She turned away from his screen and had a sip from her cappuccino. The warm froth stuck to her nose.

She was supposed to hate Max.

She knew that.

Sarah knew that, according to those with good advice like paper waste, hating Max was the only logical conclusion. After all he had done to her.

But she didn't.

Sarah put down her cup; instead she came here, morning after morning, to do the most important work she had ever done in her life, finding answers to questions that were imposing themselves.

This was the outside, but steadied.

This was the only way.

The Old World was gone and so were the pesky memories that stuck to it and here was another one and everything was beautiful, if only Peter agreed.

"So..."

Claire asked the most idiotic question on the planet exactly the way Lizzie had expected her to:

"How is everything?"

Lizzie grabbed the pint of Litovel Claire had just placed on the table in front of her and said:

"Cheers, first of all."

"Cheers."

On the wooden benches around them, everyone pretended that it was summer already.

"So?"

Strapless tops caused goose pumps next to this year's skirts and last year's sunglasses. Table for table, the pretty patio in front of The George was occupied by horn-rimmed would-bes and grey-haired have-beens and very few of those in-between, because those in-between knew, as much as Lizzie knew, that time couldn't be squandered:

Golden periods didn't last forever.

"Everything's great," Lizzie said.

She smiled.

"Things have worked out wonderfully. I'm just – hold on."

She looked at her phone.

Why now?

"One second okay?"

Claire nodded.

"Sure."

Lizzie turned away a little, picked up and said:

"Hey Jo, what's up?"

There was all sorts of noise at the other end, and Lizzie couldn't hear the caring voice she had grown used to, day after day, night after night.

"Hello?"

Claire looked as clumsy as ever; why was it that some people never changed, while others changed so much in such a stupidly short span of time?

"Lizzie?"

"I'm here, yes, what's happening?"

"Lizzie!"

"Yes, Jo."

"Lizzie..."

"Hey, I know my name, what's wrong with you? Are you drunk? Where are you?"

Claire pretended to look away; next to them, someone showed a photography portfolio to a bunch of awkwardly grinning newcomers, overdoing everything.

"I'm fucked," Jonathan said.

Lizzie turned away a little more; she hadn't heard him in this state, leaving his sentences unfinished because he had forgotten how he had started them, since that night, when, looking into his eyes for what had seemed hours, she had finally broken through the wall he had erected around himself.

When she had finally heard him whisper the words she had dreamt about hearing all those days, love on both of their lips, holding on.

And on.

And on.

When their embrace had triggered the radical transformation in Jonathan that had surprised her as much as it must have surprised him.

"Lizzie? They have fucked me, Lizzie."

"What's happening?"

Lizzie glanced back at Claire by way of sincere apologies for this embarrassment, but Claire kept smiling.

"They..."

"Hey, do you want to talk, or not? Where are you?"

"They have sacked me."

"What?"

"Yes."

"What?"

"They have fucking sacked me, Lizzie, can you believe it? They have just kicked me out..."

The music swallowed whatever else he had said.

"Where are you, Jonathan?"

"What now, Lizzie? Can you tell me that?"

"Where are you?"

"Fucking idiots, just like that... they don't even think... they have no idea how much, what... they, fucking –"

"Jonathan! Where are you?"

"I'm drinking."

"I can hear that..."

"They've sacked me, Lizzie," Jonathan said in a tone that shrivelled like a balloon losing its air.

"I'll call you back, okay?"

"No, no, don't go! I need to be with you, where are you?"

"I'm... I'm at The George, but –"

"I'm coming."

"No, but Jonathan, I'm here with Claire."

But he had hung up already.

Ready to fall through the gates of The George from wherever he was falling around now.

Lizzie turned around again.

Ready to turn a relationship that had so quickly grown so much closer than either of them could have imagined into a distraction that had the potential to kill a project that mattered more than anything.

"That didn't sound good."

How much she needed Claire now.

"No, it didn't," Lizzie said and had a large sip from her Litovel.

"Listen, Claire, I'm really sorry, but my boyfriend's lost his job. He's coming here now. He is..."

"Do you want me to leave?"

That was easy.

"No, I don't, it's just that..."

"No, Lizzie, absolutely. I understand completely. You two need to talk about this alone."

Lizzie nodded.

"Let's just meet another time, okay?" Claire said and got up.

"It's hard..."

Lizzie looked at her.

"You know, Lizzie... I know exactly what it's like, because... What can I say: I was made redundant, too."

"What?"

"I wanted to tell you later, but I might as well tell you now, right?"

"That's terrible."

Claire sat down on the edge of the bench again.

"Yes," she said.

"So what are you doing?"

"Well," she said, and:

"I'm doing what we're all doing, right? I'm moving back to my parents."

"Really?"

The great taboo.

The last resort.

The final stop in a ride that had catapulted them away from family dining tables only for them to return, cap in hand, having gained nothing at all.

"What can I do?" Claire said.

Lizzie nodded.

She could have re-pasted that part of her story: bleary-eyed knocking at a door she had feared more than anything, only to be welcomed by her mum with arms opened wider than they had ever been opened before.

She could have told the truth.

About three weeks in January that had turned December's lessons into ideas that would never have had a chance in here, the bubble, where everything got swallowed the moment it emerged.

About her time among the narrow-minded.

About a short break that had been meant to steady everything that had been stirred up by the bridge, the hospital and the rest, but had ended up handing her an ignition more powerful than any had ever been, leading her re-charged, loved-up self all the way to the Wick.

To start again.

Lizzie looked up again.

"God, sorry, Claire, I completely drifted off..."

"No worries. It's, I mean, everyone's doing it, so there's no real problem, but, God, it's so frustrating. Anyway, I don't want to be in the way when your boyfriend comes. It's important that you're there for him now. Let's meet another time, okay?"

Lizzie nodded.

It was important that she was there for him now.

Lizzie mumbled:

"Yes, let's do that. I'm sorry..."

"Don't be sorry, I hope it goes well. It's much easier to get through this as a couple. You see, I didn't have anyone. I wish I would have. It's that way to the bus stop, isn't it?"

Lizzie nodded.

"Care and attention, that's all your boyfriend needs right now."

Lizzie stared at her.

"He definitely needs you more than I need you right now," Claire said, supposedly trying to sound funny and bent down to kiss her on the cheeks.

"See you soon."

She turned around and walked through the gates and was gone, leaving Lizzie to sink underneath words that brought up the worst fear:

Care and attention.

What could she possibly do for him now, having decided what she needed to do?

Led by a force she still couldn't identify.

She had a large sip from her Litovel.

What could she possibly do for him now? Having started doing what she had to do for the first time in her life.

This wasn't working.

The entrance door to her flat looked at Sarah in anticipation, but Sarah didn't move. The key in her hand was ready to be pushed and turned, but the switch was letting her down. Sarah tried, once again, to shake it all off.

But there was simply too much ballast.

She moved the key towards the lock.

There was still simply too much excitement flowing through her body, another day spent discussing the great doing without: a collective exercise in abstaining from the luxuries everyone had come to take for granted, no questions asked.

Sarah hesitated.

This was the moment to shift the priorities back to where the priorities belonged.

She stared at her key.

This was their chance to bring back a simplicity that had long gotten lost in modern life's accepted pile of fake desires and made-up needs and if Sarah had gotten around to realising this, anybody could:

The Old World was over.

This was the moment to take a deep breath and re-consider absolutely everything and if Sarah had gotten around to grasping this, what excuse was there, not to?

The Old World was gone.

She pushed the key into the lock.

There was no time.

On the other side of the door Peter would be waiting to tell his day so he could relax for the one to follow: the professional couple was going on regardless, but today her transition walk hadn't worked.

Sarah turned the key.

Today, the street hadn't done what it was supposed to do, another abuse-screaming soul to her rescue as the anonymous masses stumbled from one collision to the next.

Wasn't everyone feeling the reflection administered from above?

Today, the impression procession hadn't done a thing.

Sarah pushed the door and entered.

Wasn't everyone feeling that there was no longer a need to cancel lunches or board a wrong bus or do any of the things that had seemed necessary to start thinking about the wider picture, because, right now, the wider picture was being pushed into everyone's face?

Sarah got out of her shoes and opened the door to their living room; wasn't everyone realising that they were all in this together now?

"Hey," she said.

Peter looked up from his paper. The used plate in front of him answered Sarah's first question.

"Sorry, I'm a bit late..." she said and took a few steps towards him.

"Oh well," he said and looked down again:

"I'm used to that by now."

Sarah placed her keys onto the table.

"Come on, it's not that bad," she said.

"I meant that in the most neutral way possible."

Peter turned a page.

"It didn't sound like that."

He looked up.

"Well, it was meant like that, but if you come in here all edgy and don't get anymore what I'm saying, that's not my fault, is it?"

"I'm not... It's just..."

A mission that couldn't be switched off, just like that.

"I know, I know... hard day and all that. You know what? You're edgier now than you used to be when you still worked for the newspaper."

Doing as asked.

Writing as told.

Living her life inside a box that had seemed to choke her a little more by the day...

"That's not true," she said and sat down on the armrest of their Chesterfield couch.

"I came in here totally relaxed... You started this."

"Started what exactly?"

Peter looked at her.

"This..."

"This, Sarah, is the way we communicate now, haven't you realised that? This, my dear, is the way we now talk."

He put away the paper and got up.

"That's not true, Peter."

He took his plate and walked past her.

"And it has been ever since you started locking yourself up all day, wherever you are locking yourself up, with that mad guy, doing whatever you guys do until the middle of the night."

"Hey, it's not the middle of the night."

Peter put his plate in the sink and turned around again.

"And then you come in here and blame me for your tensions. Think about it, Sarah."

"But..."

He opened the door to their bedroom.

"Think about it."

She had prepared, hadn't she?

She had given her best.

She had tried as hard as possible, but Peter closed the door of the bedroom behind him.

"I'm sorry," she mumbled.

Why wasn't Peter joining those that had assured her that this was a good idea?

Why wasn't he giving her the credit she deserved for this tightrope walk between two spheres in a constant quarrel, her days spent trying to wake up others from the kind of life she continued to live, once she was here?

Allocating energy in equal measures for the sake of a relationship that was too precious to be thrown away.

"Peter, I'm sorry," she said, but there was no reply. Peter had gone into protective withdrawal and who could blame him?

She got up.

Who could blame Peter for not having arrived where Sarah had arrived?

She walked to the kitchen and opened the fridge, but it seemed that her boyfriend had stopped including her in the improvised cooking that had become the awkward norm in this relationship now. She closed the door again and leaned against it backwards.

"Peter, come on, let's talk," she said, but there was no answer.

"I'm sorry..."

She turned around and opened the bottle of Shiraz that stood next to the fridge and grabbed a glass from the sink and closed her eyes and sighed.

"I'm sorry."

But she had taken a decision and there was no doubt that she was right and everyone who hadn't woken up to that truth would do so very, very soon.

These pictures made his blood circulate faster with every minute he allowed them:

"Onwards!"

Feeling the magic kick of a million others in their back, the adrenalin-fuelled frontline pressed on without fear.

"Everyone!"

There was no doubt.

The message that was being composed on his screen was entering hearts and the daring action that was required to turn this around had taken over minds.

"Now!"

Everyone out there felt that those still trying to look threatening were retreating, step by step, because they knew as much as everyone knew that the lies they were defending couldn't be defended any longer.

Max closed the door to Café Oto behind him.

Because the truth was out.

The false belief that had kept everyone from doing the right thing for too long was gone and everyone out there knew that it wouldn't take much longer for those that were still nervously clinging to their shields to turn around and join them.

He turned around the corner.

It was dark by now.

Max started walking away from the full-colour posters that proudly advertised Dalston Lane's transformation into just another street.

How much clearer could it get?

Max punched the air; glued together by a common thread for the first time in their lives, a generation no one had wanted to be a part of was about to finish off those that were still awkwardly defending the disastrous road that had led them into this mess in the first place.

"Onwards," Max mumbled, and:

"Everyone..."

But tonight, not even the sweet proof of their success was enough to push away the black top.

Max shook his head.

Not even the frontline could take away her tight white jeans, the same outfit she had worn the night Mangal had led them into her Stoke Newington flat.

Max walked faster.

He tried, once again, to feel London's heartbeat to steady his own, but not even the slideshow of shadows that ruled these parts at night managed to diffuse a connection that was worth more than anything:

Her smile.

Max followed Dalston Lane as it curved left; there was no time for this, strange parts of his body being whirled up like that, but there was nothing he could do about it.

He crossed the roundabout without looking left or right.

Sarah was closer to him than he had ever dared to imagine.

That was the issue.

Having encouraged him to go all the way with the vision that had come to him in the marshes, she was closer to him than had ever seemed possible.

"You just have to do this, Max."

He couldn't forget the words Sarah had used to follow up the most daring speech he had ever given in his life, the dull, mechanical humming of a hospital room as a backdrop, the fluorescent light as a stage light.

All their eyes had been on him, as Sarah had said:

"You just have to."

He couldn't forget how she had grabbed his arm and had looked at him in a mix of admiration and expectation as he had mumbled:

"I know, Sarah," and:

"I know."

And, for the first time in his life, he hadn't lost the idea in a negative swirl of what other people had thought, sharpened and taken forward, because she had, wide-eyed, asked him if there was anything she could do to help.

"Are you serious?"

Max punched the air again.

How far they had come, finishing off those still lying themselves through their inaction with yet another excuse to deny what couldn't be denied any longer.

How much he had achieved since he had bravely ditched the battle forever.

Max looked up.

The scenery spread, as it did every night, the sleeping train tracks giving way to the supermarket in front of a row of dark, laundry-festooned balconies, but a vague feeling of belonging in these parts wasn't enough to beat the tingle that was getting in the way, once again, without control:

Her black top.

Max rushed on.

Her tight white jeans.

He turned the corner.

Her smile.

The African shops that lined this end of Ridley Road had long been closed. The infatuation that came from large piles of plantains drenched in a biting smell of dried fish was gone. This street had turned into another place where the figures of night could come and go as they pleased, bleary-eyed mumbling to a London sky that pretended to listen to cries that really went unnoticed.

"See you tomorrow, sweetie," Max had said, but Sarah had simply ignored the final word in a carefully prepared goodbye address that had taken all his courage and days of preparation, but had yielded nothing.

"See you tomorrow, Max."

Having wrapped the bitter-sweet reminder of what had happened on her Chesterfield couch with her jumper again, she had left exactly the way she always did, packing up right at the moment they had clicked the button to beam out another rallying cry to those that were only waiting to be rallied.

And what a cracker it had been today:

"Dissidents!"

What a glorious reason to celebrate, but Sarah had simply grabbed her bag and had waved and had rushed out to sit down at a dining table in her second life and that had left Max with no other option but to point his whimsical remarks at a tired laptop screen instead.

Where the loose thoughts had stared back at him:

"Can you hear what we are hearing?"

Out there, the drawbridges were going up, but that was just another trench they would bridge. Out there, divisions were being overcome, useless tags abandoned. Old fashioned labels were being thrown away and there was no doubt where this would lead:

"Can you see them sweating?"

On the corner with St Mark's Rise, the ice cube mountains the fishmongers dumped onto the pavement night after night had melted away.

Once again, everyone was calming down, but Max:

"Are you ready?"

In front of him, the barbed wire announced the pretty Victorian house that was about to be assigned a higher purpose, but for now, provided free shelter for squatters, rats and the revolutionary core.

Max smiled.

Tomorrow he would use these lines to deliver another master stroke, but not before he had celebrated them with Sarah. Hugging her.

And never letting go.

"At home?"

"Yes, I..."

Jonathan lifted another piece of meat with the plastic fork, only to drop it again.

"For fuck's sake, I'm waiting for you at The George. Why aren't you here?"

"I... I..."

"Jesus."

"I thought you're with Claire and I didn't want to embarrass you and so I went to get some food first and..."

Soaking up the pints that had littered the way from Brick Lane to here with mushy pita bread.

"How considerate of you. I've been waiting here for almost an hour now. Alone."

"I'm so sorry, Liz, I thought..."

Only the best, more kebab salad to the rescue. The duvet of their bed was pushed aside, his shoes were lying in front of him. His eyes were still slightly out of focus, but he was getting there.

"Guess I'm coming home then?"

"No, no, I can come to you."

But Lizzie had hung up already; something was making her strangely edgy since she had started getting up before seven every morning to lock herself in her studio for the whole day, feverishly working on a so-called piece Jonathan wasn't allowed to see.

But that would surely pass.

"Alright, alright," Jonathan mumbled.

Lizzie's clothes were lying around everywhere, red vests and green leggings and comfy jumpers and tight tops and her modest make-up stood on the small table opposite and her pyjamas waited on the bed next to him and Jonathan touched them and smiled, but time was running out:

He had to get sober.

"Alright, alright," he mumbled again and picked another grilled attempt to push away the alcohol from a brown box that hadn't been handed to him by Adem, Hakan or Mustafa, but by those, whose names Jonathan hadn't learned yet.

Because Jonathan had a real home now.

Because Jonathan was here.

And he couldn't stand the old gang's accusing looks when he said what had to be said:

"I've moved, you know."

As had everyone.

"Up the road."

Trading the Ditch for Dalston; Jonathan put the box next to him and stretched.

The stray dog had jumped the bandwagon.

The stray dog had joined the caravan of hope as it had started making its way up Kingsland Road:

To fresh terrain!

To unspent ground!

Surrounded by all those that had started spitting on Mother and the rest in a belief that, up the road, a new horizon would emerge, Jonathan had walked away from his Shoreditch years with a grin.

To unseen pleasures!

Amid those exchanging one dump for another, Jonathan had smiled safe in the knowledge that, for him, the sun had already risen.

He pushed himself up from the bed.

The feeling had risen inside of him like a penis on his way to erection.

Standing in a weird morning light outside the hospital, the certainty had been too strong for him not to throw away once holy principles and finally stop denying what couldn't be denied any longer:

That this was beyond the penis.

Jonathan walked out of the bedroom; she would be here any minute now, but he was still not nearly as presentable as he would like to be.

He entered the bathroom.

Of course, it hadn't been him lying between the white sheets.

He turned on the water.

Of course, he had found the mud-covered stairs of The Bunker just in time. Of course, he had, once again, gotten away with his reckless behaviour.

Jonathan splashed two handfuls of cold water into his beer-warmed face and the shock it delivered was enough to replace these warm thoughts with a reality he had tried so hard to beat with their fail-safe help:

They had fucking sacked him.

"Shit, shit, shit."

He couldn't even afford this overpriced one-bedroom dividing line between a past and a future anymore.

"Shit."

Soon he wouldn't be able to afford anything anymore.

"Shit, shit, shit."

Jonathan dried his face and the towel's scent brought back the lingering ecstasy of last night's holding on, which had so nicely wrapped him this morning, until the pig, huffing and puffing, had ripped it away from him.

Jonathan kept breathing in.

This was the scent that kept him going, minor submissions: made.

Little admissions: done.

Having come all the way, this was the foundation that would carry him, with or without a job.

The door opened without a warning.

Lizzie said:

"Why didn't you tell me you where here?"

They had started a bond that had grown strong enough to take this head-on.

"I was just not quick enough. I..."

"Man, and open a window. Don't you smell that?"

"What?"

Lizzie rolled her eyes.

"Alright, alright."

Jonathan walked over and pushed up the sash window. The cold air tried, just the way the water had, to hit him with an inconvenient truth, but Jonathan had someone else now and that was all that mattered.

He turned around to hug Lizzie, but she backed off.

"What?" he said, and:

"Won't I get a kiss?"

She just looked at him.

"What is it, Lizzie?"

Lizzie sat down on the bed where Jonathan had sat a few minutes earlier and said, a little calmer now:

"Sit down, Jonathan," and:

"We need to talk."

Sarah's good-morning cappuccino was half cold by now, but she had a sip anyway.

She picked up her phone, only to put it down again.

The froth stuck to her lips.

Next to her, two mums moved their prams back and forth to the rhythm of Church Street, Stoke Newington; this was part of the package, taking a morning off whenever she felt like it, because Sarah was the one making the rules now.

She took up the phone again.

If only there wasn't last night's wound.

She let it sink again.

If only Peter hadn't locked himself in the bedroom, too angry to come out, and Sarah hadn't shied away from entering, too scared or proud or whatever.

Next to her small table outside The Blue Legume, two tiny hands rested on a blanket.

Two tiny eyes remained closed.

If only she hadn't spent the night on their couch, more aware with every sleepless hour that this had been a hard-to-heal scar in the making, the slow and painful withering of their base; Sarah picked up the phone again, only to feel it vibrating in her hand, but it wasn't her boyfriend that half-screamed her name on the other side:

"You can't believe the breakthrough I just had," and:

"Where are you?"

One of the mums gave her a glance that was hard to read. Sarah tried to keep her voice down.

"Hi Max," she said, and:

"I'm on Church Street. Having coffee."

"You must come in. I have to tell you about this. When can you come?"

Sarah wanted to sigh.

Next to her, a tiny head started turning a little, left and right.

"Actually, I thought of taking the day off..."

"But Sarah, this is important."

Two tiny eyes opened, slowly, totally overwhelmed by input that would only start making sense much later.

If at all.

"Can't we talk tomorrow?" she said.

"Why not now?"

Two tiny eyes squinted.

"I... I... Listen, Max, I need some time to think."

"What are you thinking about?"

Sarah didn't answer.

"This will give you something amazing to think about," Max said, and:

"What could be more important?"

Sarah bit her lip.

A conversation that had taken weird turns. A relationship that had taken the hit. A base that had to be prevented from crumbling further. Life outside of the mission.

Things Max didn't understand.

"Sarah, did you hear me?"

"It's just that..."

"What could be more important?"

"Well..."

"Please Sarah, it's so important, you know... to me."

Two tiny fingers started stretching, as if in slow motion, grabbing things that weren't actually there. Sarah kept staring at them. She didn't say anything.

"Sarah?"

"Okay, I'm coming, but give me an hour okay?"

"Okay, sure, I can't wait though. I'll see you here. I'm here. See you in a bit, okay?"

Two tiny eyes dedicated their attention to the real mum now.

"Okay," she said and hung up and placed the mobile in front of her again and picked it up immediately, no time for excuses getting in the way, and dialled and said:

"Hey..."

But Peter said:

"It's not a great time, Sarah."

"I know, I'm sorry, I shouldn't call you at work, but I just thought –"

"Well, yeah, but I have to go."

"I'm just... I'm sorry for yesterday and I was wondering if we could go for dinner tonight, you know, somewhere close, just the way we used to and –"

"I have to call you back."

And that was that.

He had hung up. Sarah lowered her arm. Engaged by another meeting, delivering another project. Satisfying another demand to the very best of his abilities.

Sarah had another sip.

And another.

On the table, her phone vibrated.

That was quick.

"Fancy meeting for a coffee? xx"

She shook her head.

That wasn't Peter.

That was Jonathan, asking for what she had been so happy to give and take for months now, as the four of them had tried to process events like one happy family, making sense of what had started in Mangal and had covered that whole, terrible night until a hospital room had multiplied it by the factor ten, their awkward hesitancy to touch each other, taken...

But she had no time for this now.

What had happened was well documented; the feeling as little understood as it was then.

But this wasn't the right moment.

The boy that had started to rest his head on a pillow next to Lizzie would have to wait and respect that a certain sense of normality had taken over, four people going about their ways; Sarah picked up the phone to text a polite apology, but before she could even start, Jonathan ditched the easy-way-out communication that was texting and said:

"Sarah, I'm sorry to call, but it's... I need someone to talk to. Everything's going all wrong again. Where are you?"

Why was everyone so demanding today?

"What's up?"

"I'm feeing terrible, I lost my job, shit... and.. and.. I have to tell you in person..."

Lost his job?

"It's about Lizzie..." he said.

Lost Lizzie?

"Oh my God..."

"Yeah."

Had he been betraying her? The move wasn't easy, switching from targeting all to being bound to just one; the road was littered with failures.

"Are you okay?"

"Hardly."

But why was she the one who had to deal with this?

"Can we meet tomorrow?"

"No, but I need someone now... I..."

Wasn't it time she stopped playing the mother for the likes of Jonathan, lost souls in the city's relentless stream, and started being a mother for someone that really needed one?

Next to her, two tiny eyes were wide awake by now.

"I'm about to meet Max at Café Oto. We —"

"Can I come?"

"What, to our —"

"Yeah, why not? It would be nice to see Max too. I just need someone around me."

Sarah didn't say anything.

"It's all going wrong again, Sarah," and:

"Please, can I come?"

They never had anyone around: it was always just Max and Sarah, their mission and them.

"I don't know what Max would say..."

"Ah Maxo, he will be fine. Thanks so much, Sarah."

She hadn't even agreed, but hearing the relief in his voice prevented her from objecting now.

"Well, okay. I'll see you there in one and a half hours, okay? There are a few things that —"

"Okay great," he said and hung up and, once again, Sarah let her arm sink slowly.

She leaned back.

It wasn't a bad idea, actually.

She would listen to Max and approval-nod him through his breakthrough, and then she would listen to Jonathan and sympathy-smile him through his story, whatever his story was, and then she would go home and get ready for Peter and their time at whichever restaurant he would choose.

And Jonathan could stay with Max and get his void filled with a message perfectly suited for filling voids like that.

After all, he was perfect material, wasn't he?

These lines would do it.

Max teetered forward and back; out there, the megaphones were on. The entire city was filled with anger and these words would deliver the final push.

He grabbed the table for hold.

The entire city was being shaken by their chants, everyone singing from one sheet, and there was no doubt that the composition coming along on his screen was exactly what was needed, out there:

The masses wanted more.

Max started biting his fingernails as he read again:

"It starts in your head..."

This was the push that would bring all those on board that were still trying to resist.

"...and takes you here."

This was jerking up the volume.

"Where we all are."

This message would spread like a virus and penetrate every last inch of a withering era, millions about to be caught in a spell that was far too powerful to be brushed off. Masks were useless, running would be in vain.

Max leaned back and smiled.

Café Oto was surprisingly empty for a Tuesday morning. One other laptop glowed in the semi-darkness of the far corner, but all other tables were still unoccupied. No one could see the sweat that was, once again, running down his forehead.

"Where would you rather be?"

Max grabbed the half-empty cup in front of him and had a few large sips to continue covering up another night spent half-awake pushing this mission towards its only outcome.

No sleep till victory.

No sleep till this was done.

Max lowered the cup again; he needed all the caffeine he could get, but no coffee in the world was stronger than the proof that kept it all going:

"Our time is now."

Out there, the frontline was prepared to stand firm until the last exhausted body would fall, arms stretched towards the sky in a final act of deference:

That was the commitment now.

That was the bond, marching on, hand in hand, into a world worth living in.

December had smashed their opportunities, but here they were, fired, once again, by a voice everyone was dying to hear by now.

Where the hell was Sarah?

Max scrolled up.

He couldn't wait to show her how another post was turning into the kind of unashamed propaganda they had envisaged from the beginning:

"Everything can be touched."

What was taking her that long?

"Everything can be re-written."

And scrolled down again.

"All the things everyone has always accepted as God-given, can be re-configured to finally serve those they are meant to serve; everything is up for grabs."

And down.

"Nothing is holy anymore."

Max looked at his watch again.

Wasn't that so clear to see?

Next to him, a few newspapers piled, providing the kind of lame-duck thinking he was using as a springboard for his attacks: the mainstream theatre, where lying and denying took centre stage only for a whole auditorium of brain-washed conventionalists to clap their polite applause.

Ha!

A pathetic carnival of sorts that kept answering questions no one had seen before with answers everyone had been violently sick with for decades.

Was it really that hard to understand?

Max leaned back.

Was it really that difficult to get what he and Sarah were getting?

He sighed.

Oh, Sarah...

Max opened a new document and typed, losing all his focus within a few seconds:

"Dear Sarah."

Again.

"This is the letter never sent. This is everything I always wanted to tell you, but never dared."

His fingers slipped.

He knew that saying what he really wanted to say would destroy everything he had.

He rushed up.

And he couldn't risk that; he stormed away, around the table and past the worn-out couch and through the entrance door and onto the street, hectically breathing the fresh air to push this away, overused re-assurance in a calm-down loop:

Sarah was with him.

All was good.

He leaned against the stone wall behind him, if this wasn't handled with care, it could knock him out without a warning, The Elderfield in a terrible comeback. The energy he had gained in the marshes powered this dream duo, but the bond that had come as a result was covered by a fear that wouldn't leave:

Because without her, there was nothing.

"Hey Maxo!"

What the hell? Max leaned forward; was that really him, striding towards Café Oto with his usual swagger?

"Hey, old terrorist, what's up?" Jonathan said and held out his hand.

"I'm not a terrorist," Max said.

"Just joking."

They shook hands.

"Very funny."

He had no time for this at all.

"What are you doing here?" Max said; he had to impress Sarah with the latest fruits of his writing, no rules learned and all styles broken.

"It's a free street, isn't it?" Jonathan said.

"Yes, but..."

He had to soak up her smiles in admiration.

"Truth is, I'm here to see you. And Sarah."

"What?"

"Yep, I just talked to her on the phone. She said it's okay to pop around, say hello."

"Really?"

Jonathan nodded and said:

"Drink?"

Max stared at him. What the hell was he thinking, crashing their mission without a hint of respect?

"It's 11 in the morning, Jonathan."

"I know."

Jonathan grinned a stupid grin; keeping the four of them together was in the interest of Max, as much as it was in Jonathan's or anyone's, for what had happened had happened and that meant what it meant, but that didn't require Jonathan to start coming here.

"Did Sarah really say that?"

"What?"

"That you can come around."

"Yes, definitely, but I'm going to get a beer. I'll tell you everything afterwards. Fucked up shit, I tell you."

Max shook his head.

"And I thought you had changed," he said, but Jonathan had already pushed the door.

What the hell was he thinking, spoiling the moment Max had spent hours waiting for?

He fell back against the wall.

How could Sarah have allowed Jonathan to break into what they had created for themselves alone?

Lizzie pushed away a charred plank of wood and sat down cross-legged on the concrete. In front of her, the canal kept away the zone's deconstruction that was going on the other side, its dust beaten, momentarily, by a smell of sludge. There she was, content amid the lousy decade's debris.

Lizzie raised her chin.

There she was: happy amid ruins.

She leaned back.

Over there, the diggers were turning this no man's land into everyone's, but until this forgotten part of town would be at the centre of the world's attention, it belonged to them: stubborn creators, outlaws, gangs.

Until then, it was theirs.

Until the wrecking ball would hit, Lizzie could use this rubbish-strewn sanctuary, half-empty shells occupied by all those that, like her, had arrived.

She started smiling.

This was it, her brave attempt to silence the calls.

A lifetime spent slithering through this world's fake fantasia of choice was being replaced with a single decision, all uncertainties brushes aside:

This was it, her Great Project.

She was cutting herself loose from everything that had held her back for too long.

This was it.

She was killing all that wasn't needed to make way for what really counted and that, for now, was just herself, and the result was obvious, wasn't it?

In there, energy was flowing exactly where it was meant to flow, finally.

In there, inspiration was being transformed without a delay.

In there, Lizzie was reaping the return due for liberating this mind from a drink-fuelled succession of catch-up, match-up, the pubs of East London as her living room and not a chance, trapped inside a never-ending chain of shit-chat, tit-bit, hob-nob, sob-sob.

What courage!

She was breaking the self-created cobweb, a hundred drivel feeds choked with a single courageous click: the so-called social network was losing its grip.

The final update had gone out to no one, but Lizzie.

What a stroke!

She had laughed all the way to the Wick, as the chants had faded:

The chorus that had the power to paralyse even the strongest was losing its meaning.

Lizzie couldn't stop smiling.

Out here, all that was expected was down to her and Jonathan had to understand that the other night had only been the final step in a long list of necessary actions to stop the grouching, so that Lizzie could do what had to be done.

She stretched.

Over there, the bulldozers were connecting the Wick to the world. Battalions of diggers were breaking a spell that had lasted ever since the first breakneck artists had arrived, thorium for water, and had locked themselves inside a danger zone while the world had still been at peace. Living, by their own personal choice, in a constant state of emergency, while the world had swayed on sedately.

But now the Wick was being tamed.

Now, the state of emergency was everywhere, but Lizzie had found her way to deal with that reality properly and her piece was coming together beautifully.

She closed her eyes.

There it was again.

She kept them closed.

Somewhere inside of her, the sensation of her self-imposed situation was taking over the steering wheel and a slow prickling in her veins was, once again, giving way to a funny feeling, somewhere in her stomach, and it got a little stronger, every time it happened, crawling up slowly, from her toes and all the way to her forehead:

The being here.

It was rising, unstoppably:

The being alive.

And every time it happened, it got a little more beautiful, taking over every last part of her re-charged body to lead her, gently, into a land where all the sounds faded and everything turned white and nothing caused a stir at all...

Lizzie opened her eyes again.

She grabbed the rollie she had prepared for herself, lit up and dragged hectically, a harsh reality returned by nicotine:

Jonathan had to understand.

She exhaled through her nose. The smoke dissolved as if it had never been there.

That this wasn't personal at all.

"What do you mean, Lizzie?" he had said after she had finished with her carefully worded request for a distance she needed more than anything right now.

"I mean just that."

Jonathan had to understand that this was simply the final step in a breakout that allowed Lizzie to listen to a voice she had never heard before.

"But..."

That, protected from life's accepted assault of distraction by a thundering A12, she could finally listen to herself.

She had another drag.

That there was no way she could let this pass.

"But..."

Surrounded by meaningless fragments that acquired a new meaning inside her studio, Lizzie was finally channelling everything that had to be channelled, and, for the first time in her life, that was no one's achievement, but her own.

"What's not to understand?"

In front of her, her phone was ringing again.

Lizzie sighed.

Hadn't she been clear enough, all energy summoned to explain exactly what was behind her decision?

"Jonathan," she mumbled.

Was there really a need to torture her like that and make her go through it all over again?

"Don't be so cruel."

Lizzie pressed red.

He had to understand that the flow could die any minute.

"Please don't..."

Lizzie threw her half-finished cigarette into the algae-covered water in front of her and got up.

Her time was now.

Wasn't that clear?

She stepped over a leaking canister and started striding, her eyes back in focus, through the ashes and towards a sun that was getting stronger by the day.

Golden periods didn't last forever.

It was that simple.

"Didn't I say in one and a half hours?"

Sarah lowered her bag onto the outside table that divided her from Max and him.

"Well, yeah," Jonathan said; but his fucked-up situation surely justified the exception, didn't it?

Sarah crossed her arms.

"In fact, Max was just telling me about your mission and how it's happening out there big time, and –"

"Was he?"

Jonathan nodded; yesterday's succession of shit clearly meant that it was okay to disrupt this pathetic little attempt to save the world from a café table.

"That's right Max, isn't it? You were just saying about the millions out there..."

But Max didn't answer.

Max looked at Sarah, but Sarah only said:

"I don't have much time."

Jonathan grabbed his empty glass from the table in between them and said:

"Drink anyone?"

"Jesus," Max said and he and Sarah exchanged a look Jonathan couldn't quite read.

"What?"

Behind Sarah, another drunk staggered to the construction work's unsteady rhythm.

Jonathan looked away.

A chilly breeze whirled a plastic bag through the otherwise empty side street that housed Café Oto.

"Alright, alright..." he said, and:

"I'll wait a little longer."

Only one person was missing to make this encounter what it used to be.

But that was the whole problem.

One like all.

Only one person was missing to bring back a magic that was impossible to describe, the four of them standing in a circle, once again:

All like one.

Only Lizzie could make this good again and return what had to come back, the sense of a connection deeper than anything any of them had ever felt, but Lizzie had broken away from this, and that left Jonathan with no choice but to grab what remained:

"So what was it about jobs you wanted to say earlier, Max?"

Jonathan looked at Max, but Max was still weirdly fixated on Sarah. He said, without intonation at all:

"Well, we're all going to have several of them very soon. But this isn't the right time –"

Jonathan snorted.

"Several, eh? I don't even have one anymore."

"What I mean is that we're all going to share the work that's necessary for a functioning society between all of us and because that will give us financial stability, we will all have the time and money to do all the things we also like to do. How beautiful is that?"

"Right," Jonathan said.

It was hard not to mock this, Max having figured out everything, once again.

"Everyone contributes. Everyone benefits."

But this was a lifeline:

Could he get some of that fire?

Max waited for a response.

But Sarah didn't answer, so Jonathan said, his empty pint still in hand:

"Yeah, but who decides what's needed for society?"

Max turned at him.

Could he have a slice of meaning?

"Well, someone has to decide, obviously."

Max turned away again.

"Max, the tyrant, eh?" Jonathan said and shook his head a little; was he really following up three pints and a line sniffed out of the secret reserve he kept from his past with a serious conversation involving Max, the dreamer, about the deceiving illusion everyone kept calling society? Was that really what he had come to?

"It would all happen within the boundaries of that over-hyped product called western liberal democracy."

"Blah blah."

"It's just that they're all wimps."

Max almost shouted this.

"It's just that everyone's a bloody coward."

He banged his fist on the table.

"Yeah!" Jonathan shouted, because that was more like it.

"Damn right."

Because this was about the pigs, huffing and puffing, and about being fucked over in the most brutal way and dreaming, thinking, talking never got anywhere at all.

"That's a bit harsh, isn't it?" Sarah said.

Max stared at her.

"No, it's not too harsh... Anyway, when have you started being on the other side, Sarah? First it takes you ages to get here and then you're arguing against me."

Max looked as if he was regretting the words as he said them.

"Excuse me?"

Jonathan put down his empty glass again.

"When has arguing become a crime?" Sarah said.

Max didn't reply.

"I'm not even arguing, I'm just... Anyway... I can come and go whenever I want to, right?"

"Yeah, but –"

"No but. What you sometimes fail to see, Max, is that other people still have a life to live out there."

She grabbed her bag.

"Anyway, I'm off now, because I'm going for dinner with Peter tonight."

She turned around.

"See you guys soon."

Jonathan could only watch, as the actual reason for this meeting disappeared towards Kingsland High Street:

A little female sympathy.

A sweet pick-me-up from someone who continued to be more than a little special.

A word of motherly advice.

Jonathan turned around to look at Max.

"So there we are."

But Max just stood there, staring through the large window into the dim café, where a lonely laptop was sitting on an otherwise empty table.

"Hey!"

But Max didn't react.

As if someone had switched him off.

"You were telling me something about real action, Max. Remember?"

But Max just kept staring.

As if something inside of him had just died.

"Hey man," Jonathan said.

"Action."

He took out his mobile, but there was still no reply, five text messages in vain and no other way to get to her, locked away inside a studio whose location she hadn't given away, not even yesterday night, as she had high-pitch justified her ridiculous behaviour with reasons that hadn't made any sense to Jonathan at all.

He needed another drink.

Had Lizzie forgotten the boldness of his move, having left everything behind to stride, hand in hand, through the couple land he now called home?

Only to end up jobless, loveless, done.

He needed so much more.

"You still want to hear about it?"

Jonathan looked up.

"Still alive, then?" he said and Max nodded.

"I would love to hear about it, man," Jonathan said, and: "Drink?"

And Max nodded again.

Sarah looked at the red dress in her hand. That would be a bit over the top, wouldn't it?

She pushed it back in.

Peter had sounded far less excited about the fact that they were having dinner than he had about having some news he had refused to give away over the phone:

"I'll tell you tonight."

Others might be jittering, but Peter was safe, having moved as asked, done as told. No one was getting rid of a poster child like that easily, and no one was benefiting from that more than Sarah.

She slid open another door.

She hadn't touched these piles in ages: colour-fading, moth-threatened remainders of a time when it had been okay to buy and throw.

Get and forget.

When it had been perfectly fine to carry her wage through the tempting entrances of the city's brightly lit sanctuaries, every denomination catered for.

All credit cards accepted.

But that was in the Old World.

That was over; Sarah took out a pair of blue jeans. Wouldn't that do for tonight?

Peter had suggested Yum Yum, after all, where you sat comfortably and without your shoes on. Sarah threw the trousers over her arm. These were simple, but suitable, which, of course, was exactly what this was all about, shopping postponed until the mission had become what it was meant to become.

She smiled.

All that wasn't needed shed for a life that made more sense with every day she contemplated it.

Everyone was waking up to what Hackney had been doing for ages, unwanted items put on the street for those who thought differently to pick them up.

Everyone was going down a gear and Sarah was right in the middle of it all.

She threw the jeans onto the bed behind her and went through a pile of tops.

Sarah was at the heart of an operation that would convert everyone who wasn't converted yet: to live on less, swapping clothes and sharing skills and growing what could be grown, cutting back on everything that still prevented the deep breath that had carried her to the precious space she now occupied.

Sarah picked up a black top.

Poor Max.

She hadn't meant to leave him like that, but he had hardly left her a choice, had he, barking the way he had? Once again, losing all his respect in a torrent of passion that was nothing but admirable, spouting a half-baked theory in full expectation that everyone would love it:

His drive was inhuman.

His focus was adorable, but sometimes it was hard to handle the result as he steamed on, forever tortured by worries that he wasn't making enough progress in the short span of time he had given himself.

Black and blue would be a little too dark, wouldn't it?

Tonight was meant to be a re-union, after all.

This was meant to be a meal to heal the scar and Sarah was looking forward to it more than she had looked forward to anything in many, many weeks.

She put the top back onto the pile.

Max had to understand.

He had simply been trapped for too long, waiting and watching as the clocks had ticked into his head the conviction that the system wasn't working, because it didn't allow people like him to live up to their potential.

Sarah went through another pile.

Max had to understand that most people needed a little longer to wake up from the Old World's deceit, because they had only just started realising what Max had mapped out a long time ago.

That most people were only just embarking on a journey Max was right in the middle of, a lifetime of preparation.

A wild mind that had no other concerns.

A magic that couldn't be described and a determination that still had the power to scare her more than a little:

For the mission, Max was prepared to do anything.

But the statistics calmed him down and the statistics were in Sarah's hands.

Which was another issue altogether...

Sarah let her fingers glide from the top shelf to what used to be her everyday, a hundred tones of grey in one orderly line. These clothes hadn't been touched since that night in December.

She moved them along the rack.

Hanger for hanger, these were the bittersweet memories of touching in and of touching out. A life in perfect order, until a telephone interview that had been meant to be just a telephone interview had started what had taken her here, freed from the inside in a way no one had expected, least of all herself.

Sarah shuddered.

The Old World with its last terrible roar. Something she wanted to forget forever.

Sarah took out a blouse in red and green; there was no need to think about it any more:

The only ones that were still shaking their heads were those that kept clinging to the Old World's outmoded categories, when everyone else was moving on.

Sarah put down the blouse on top of the jeans.

The only ones that were still raising their eyebrows were those that were losing.

And soon, they, too, would get rescued.

Soon enough, they, too, would arrive, where Sarah had arrived. Where, if only they dared, they could find themselves, just like her.

Sarah slumped onto their bed.

Woken from their past.

She leaned back and eyed the red dress again, squeezed in between her work clothes and the casual stuff she was wearing for their mission.

She could take Peter for a walk through Clissold Park afterwards, couldn't she?

They hadn't done that in ages.

If they kept on their jackets, they could even have a glass of wine in their garden, talking life, talking love...

There was a whole life to be enjoyed, wasn't there?

Sarah got up and took out the dress again and stripped it off its hanger.

Max pressed red.

There was as much point explaining the mission to his parents as there had been explaining the battle; Max pushed the mobile into his pocket.

Explaining what he was all about now would be wasted energy: a long distance call, where half the information was lost. A conversation, where two languages were being spoken, no translator present.

They were simply too far away from this.

Max kept walking.

Those shielding themselves from the bad news with a garden fence demanded clarity, but, unfortunately, what happened inside of Café Oto didn't fit their patterns. Those shutting away the bigger picture because it ran the danger of destroying the idyll they had created for themselves wanted something they could relate to:

A tag.

A lie.

A label, but unfortunately Max had decided otherwise and parental approval had never been sought for this, his life dedicated to a higher cause, because Max knew that, sooner or later, his parents would feel the heat too.

That, sooner or later, the bigger picture would crash into their living rooms like a hand grenade.

Around Max were the crumbling Victorian houses that dominated the upper end of St Mark's Rise, long staircases leading to red doors, a black cat parading a wall that had seen better days. But the street lamps weren't nearly bright enough to shock Max back into focus, a mind caught by events that wouldn't leave:

Stupid idiot, Jonathan.

Entering, without a hint of shame, what no one had been meant to enter. Breaking what had seemed unbreakable, because he had deemed it necessary to push his drunken, disorderly self in between Max and Sarah.

Spoiling a conversation he had no place in; was it really a surprise that Lizzie had dumped him, if his promise to have changed still left him with no idea about the world beyond his early morning pint?

And still: he had listened.

"That's very interesting."

A new drink in hand, he had nodded.

"Tell me more."

It had been quite a surprise: eyes opened wide, Jonathan had demanded what Max had never given to anyone. Nervously tapping his feet to music that hadn't been there, Jonathan had begged for words that had never made their way into his mouth, leaving Max exhausted, but strangely satisfied.

But Jonathan wasn't the reason Max tried so hard to get these streets to distract him.

Sarah had left a crack that prevented all progress, a whole day spent chewing the same lazy phrases, another lame cliché. A whole day spent typing and sweating, but not a single fresh thought, no headway at all.

Left alone, left behind.

The theory he had thought would resolve the eternal problem, everyone being too complex and with too much to give for the standard set-up: discredited, debunked, fouled. A mean addition to the painful, nagging doubt that could only be kept at bay by the very person who had turned around without a second glance today.

Max kicked away an empty packet of crisps.

This crack wouldn't go, however hard he tried to sum up their success, once again, in a slideshow of flags and fists and sweat and shouts and anger that was only coming out because of what they were putting out there, but the usual film wasn't coming on. Its hero was on a break, forced by a partner that hadn't even said goodbye.

"Damn it," Max mumbled.

On his left, they were both fast asleep, the caff that sold grease to long-haired pavement philosophers and the newsagent that didn't sell much to anyone, but took it with a smile that was warmer than anyone's around here.

Max had no idea what time it was.

Because time was irrelevant.

The mobile phone in his pocket vibrated just as he crossed a forsaken Shacklewell Lane.

Max stopped at the beginning of the small side street that went off just opposite the former warehouse-turned-studio space, where light still marked the big-window spaces that belonged to obsessed night workers like him.

He read:

"Hi Max, I'm sorry I behaved a little strange this morning."

He smiled.

He started walking again.

He read:

"But there are a lot of things on my mind right now."

What?

"I think I might need some time for myself right now. I have to think some things through."

What?

"I will be in touch in a few days or so."

Max let the mobile sink.

"Keep going."

The unlit fronts that flanked this narrow side street, a new development pitched against a rotting estate as so often in these parts, seemed to be moving in on him. These walls were squeezing him, The Elderfield and what had followed in a terrible re-play:

Time to think things through?

His heartbeat took over; he crossed Arcola Street at the side street's end without looking left or right and let his hands glide along the cold metal lattice that protected the basketball ground of another estate like a prison.

Everything was fine.

Max looked up.

Swathes of white smoke veiled the street, as usual, the Turkish grills doing their best to obscure the Arcola Theatre and themselves to anyone who wasn't meant to enjoy their pleasures.

Everything was good:

His partner was taking a few days off and she would return refreshed.

That was all.

Sarah took a well-deserved break and she would return strengthened.

That was clear.

The message had arrived un-xxxed, but that didn't mean anything. It had been brief, either heavily edited, or not at all, but that didn't change the one basic truth Max could be sure about:

"I will be in touch in a few days."

Ready to finally turn the mission into a movement that would change the world forever.

At its end, Arcola Street gave way to the glaring lights of Stoke Newington High Street, where the layers of night-time noise made up the reassuring soundtrack that could mean anything or nothing.

Sarah would be back just in time for a final chain reaction that would start with those lying on the ground; returned ready to see all those signed up that were still denying the fact that millions were on the streets already.

Max stopped.

If they had the likes of Jonathan on board, what could possibly stop them?

Fucking moron, Max.

It was three days ago now, but what Max had told him wouldn't leave.

He inhaled.

Stupid dreamer; Jonathan shook his head. He was hiding behind sunglasses, even though there was no hangover to conceal; the continuous feed that was in charge, once again, was leaving no ups, or downs, or anything and anyway:

Whom was he to hide a hangover from?

He was hiding behind sunglasses, even though the sun still hadn't won the fight.

The early afternoon beer garden of The White Hart was deserted, all the wooden tables occupied by ashtrays alone. In the far corner, a premature sprinkler anticipated better times, revealing tops and short skirts and ice-cold Cider, but all that was a distant dream.

Didn't Max get this?

Always just dreaming, thinking, talking, but never acting; not even able to tell Sarah what he really wanted, which was to fuck her day and night.

"Loser," Jonathan mumbled.

And still.

What he had told him inside his café three days ago didn't leave, not even now. The words were still sticking out of a blur Jonathan was once again creating for himself in a fake belief that it would heal the wounds:

"This is the time to fight back, Jonathan."

The words were still haunting him.

Wherever he chose to sit around and stare and smoke and drink, this was still on:

"This is the time to beat them."

And:

"Together we're strong."

Against the pigs, huffing and puffing, who had taken what had so clearly belonged to him, before Lizzie had followed suit; Jonathan picked up his phone again and dialled her number again, but, again, there was only a dialling tone, again and again, until the phone switched to the voicemail that had already heard a hundred of his desperate, whimpering messages.

Jonathan inhaled and exhaled.

The girl that had refused to play by the rules from the beginning was breaking them once again.

Having lured Jonathan into the kind of behaviour he had never thought possible, shell-shocked, considering for the first time in ages, that perhaps, just perhaps, love really was the answer, was that her way of showing gratitude?

Jonathan inhaled.

And exhaled; having tempted Jonathan to replace the sticky floors of Shoreditch with the tame tables of pubs the stray dog would never have dared to enter, was that the answer? Having embraced everything he used to despise, parading togetherness through The White Hart and The Red Lion and even The fucking Elderfield.

Jonathan stubbed out his cigarette.

He grabbed the pack and took out another, lit and inhaled:

Deeper.

Further.

Higher, but all this didn't feel the way it had felt before the extremes had been ironed out to allow a life that had been good, until the one that had brought it along had pissed off in the name of art.

Shit.

Smugly smiling at whatever she was smiling at, while Max and Sarah were stupidly smiling at each other over their attempt to mobilise the masses to do something the lame masses would never do.

Or were there really millions?

The thing was this:

He had some ideas, Max. If you cut through the blathering about renegotiating humankind's place on the planet and the scaremongering images, the whole world drowning in its own shit, and his screwed-up vision for something he called global justice without even the hint of irony, there was something.

Jonathan inhaled.

If you cut to the core.

And exhaled.

If you got right to the heart of the matter, there was something, but Max was going down the wrong way completely, wasn't he?

He shook his head.

"Come on, Lizzie."

Jonathan picked up his phone again and dialled but, once again, there was only this fucking dialling tone, again and again, until the phone switched to a voicemail that was already overflowing with:

"Please pick up."

If she had really meant all the things she had told him after the hospital, two weak bodies clinging to one another surrounded by kebab boxes and empty bottles of wine and a hundred cum-clotty tissues next to cold slices of pizza, she would be here for him now, wouldn't she?

"Lizzie…"

If she had really meant what they had whispered as the fucking had become love-making, two fallen angels in a tight embrace, she wouldn't prefer sleeping on the floor of whatever rubbish tip she was working in to the bed they were meant to share, would she?

"Please pick up the phone."

All of which went to say that love really was the illusion Jonathan had always thought it was.

He looked at the empty glass in front of him.

He needed another drink, but if he carried on like this, the money wouldn't carry him much further than this, a never-ending parade of pay checks having been slashed without regard:

The show was over.

In Brick Lane, the lemmings were staring themselves into decay without him, his computer having been reset, one button, no trace, and Jonathan had no other choice but to push himself from pint to pint, because there was nothing else he could fill his days with:

Why, if his job had only been there to pay for the rest, did it leave this massive void, now that it was gone?

Jonathan clutched the empty glass in front of him.

Max was right.

All of this wasn't working.

All of this was wrong.

Up there, they could do whatever they wanted to do. Up there, those that had started this terrible downward slope were still grinning, but, down here, thousands were reeling like Jonathan, all of which was to say that Max was right:

Something had to be done.

Only that Max was going down the wrong track completely; didn't he get it?

Hiding inside that dark café with Sarah.

Only that Max had no idea.

"Idiot," Jonathan mumbled, stumped out his cigarette and fumbled for another one.

Day after day, kidding himself.

Words?

Jonathan lit up and inhaled.

Deeper.

And deeper; words would never change a fucking thing. That much was clear.

Lizzie threw.

This was it, confusion being grabbed by its throat and smashed to the ground.

Another piece of broken glass was in place.

This was it, confusion being kicked, again and again, to make it pay, once and for all, for the pain it had created, smugly holding on to its upper hand:

The inside and the outside battling it out at her cost.

Lizzie grabbed the brush with the glue again and whirled around; this was it, the indecision that had paralysed her for so long, being shattered into a thousand pieces that were no more substantial than the dust that surrounded her studio.

Almost no trace.

Almost nothing left; with every fragment Lizzie threw at the new centre of her universe, the space she was creating inside her mind was growing a little bigger.

She started brushing.

For fuck's sake.

She looked at the display; there was no other way. She picked up and shouted:

"Will you stop calling me!"

She squeezed the mobile between her ear and her shoulder. Her hands kept applying the glue.

"But Lizzie!"

Every brushstroke firmed up her creation.

"I mean how selfish is all this?" he barked.

Every brushstroke created space for more.

"Can't you understand how much I need you right now? Why can't I come around?"

Lizzie lowered her brush and took the phone into her hand properly.

"I told you why."

"I will just sit there and watch, I promise. It's just that... I can't... I need you. There, I said it again. Lizzie, I need to see you, otherwise..."

"Otherwise what?"

There was a short pause.

"You have no idea what it feels like, all day long doing nothing."

She knew exactly what it felt like. But for her, that state had been replaced with a vision.

How hard was it to understand that?

"Lizzie, you have no idea what it feels like, being so... so lonely. For fuck's sake. Are you still there?"

"Yes."

"Do you know what I mean. I'm just... it's... I'm thinking all these things and... Fuck."

"What are you on?"

"What?"

"Where are you anyway?"

"In the pub. Where else can I go?"

Jesus.

"What else am I supposed to do, eh? I'm totally fucked up and you're complaining that I'm not sitting at the kitchen table doing crosswords."

The way her piece towered in front of her was almost enough to make it all fade away.

"What else am I supposed to do?"

Further and further.

"I lost my job, I lost my girlfriend. What do you expect me to do instead of this?"

And further.

"Can you tell me that?"

"Don't scream at me. God, you're so drunk."

Lizzie took a step away from it.

"Yes, I'm fucking drunk, so what?"

"Why don't you see some people? I'm not the only person on the planet, am I?"

"Well..."

Why didn't Jonathan understand that, once she was finished inside here, nothing would be lost, while everything would be gained.

"Don't be such a clinging baby! And anyway, you promised me you wouldn't do coke anymore and now you're doing coke for breakfast, is that it?"

"And? So what! I need you Lizzie."

"You don't know what you need."

"I'm... fuck. I fucking need... something," he said, and:

"Anything!"

"Exactly," Lizzie said and hung up; she bent down to place the mobile in front of her and, with a gentle kick, sent it sliding across the linoleum floor and into the far corner of her studio, where it came to a halt in an awkward silence.

As if it felt ashamed that it had allowed this distraction into the holy hall of creation.

Lizzie slid onto her knees and relaxed her legs.

Wasn't this obvious?

In her lap, her fingers stiffened; didn't Jonathan know, as much as she knew, that she had learned all this the hard way?

She stretched her fingers.

That she had been that close, stranded on Kingsland Road where the street crossed the canal, no longer able to explain herself to anyone and not even able to explain herself to herself anymore.

Ready to let go.

Prepared to jump into the dark void that had stretched below her and get dragged down, a line-up of failure tied to her weak body like a necklace of bricks. Fully convinced that the canal was deep enough to do her the favour.

Ha!

Of course, she hadn't done it.

Lizzie looked at her hands.

Of course, she hadn't won: In a final act of defeat, she had shied away even then, crouched clueless, her shivery back against the stone wall, until someone carrying a hundred better reasons to behave like her had shaken Lizzie out of her ridiculous state:

Spare the change, but spare yourself.

Of course, she hadn't done it and the strange unease about her inaction had long made way for a powerful feeling of pride, not to have been fished out by some insomniac local, a wet bundle of naivety on a hook.

Not to have humiliated herself like that.

She pushed herself up; not to have been the one to deliver December's biggest cliché.

Lizzie walked towards the window.

She opened it.

Outside, the diggers and the birds were battling it out again. Another whiff of spring brought on flip-flop strolls in flower skirts and long evenings spent relaxing winter's tension with plastic cup lager, but, for once, Lizzie was dealing with winter's tension properly, killing the question marks that had ruled her life for too long by creating what she was creating.

She looked at her piece.

Sticking them right in there, all the petty, nagging hundreds that had kept her back for so long.

Never to return.

With every piece of plastic she stuck into a new place, another one was being eradicated and the feeling of liberation it caused was stronger than anything Lizzie had ever felt.

She closed her eyes.

If only there wasn't this new question mark.

She opened them again immediately; it knocked more often now, in moments like this, when everything faded and all turned white and nothing caused a stir at all...

Shamelessly filling the space Lizzie had created.

The one that was endlessly postponed; Lizzie grabbed her pack to beat this attack with nicotine.

The one that was usually buried.

Sarah picked up another black olive from the silver plate in front of her and started chewing.

And chewing.

And chewing; what Peter had told her during their shared dinner was still only arriving, even though their planned re-union was three days ago now. The words that had followed his flattering reward for an afternoon spent in front of the wardrobe were only just gaining their full significance.

Sarah lifted up a spoon of red Turkish lentil soup, only to let it sink again.

She took a deep breath.

"They have asked me to go to Berlin again, Sarah."

"That's great."

"Yeah, but this time it's permanent."

Sarah spat the olive stone onto the silver plate; she could still see how Peter's face had morphed from widely enthusiastic to deadly serious, as he had taken her hand:

"So are you coming with me?"

A simple question.

A simple answer?

A straight-forward affair; Sarah's gaze drifted from her plate to the window that made Somine such a great place to watch the junction, humming on, and to all those on their daily stride in confidence, from office chairs to couches, running into those that, with their heads towards the pavement, had no other plans than to cross this street.

How could he have disturbed her perfect situation?

Out there, Dalston's evening parade was on, all shades of life running into each other without a shrug, but Sarah still only saw Peter looking at her:

"So?"

He was reaping the benefit of a life spent on the inside and he was offering her a part.

"So."

Sarah sighed.

She leaned back and looked around the buzzing room she had chosen for tonight's escape from her comfort zone: next to her, the smiley-faced waiters in their white shirts served a bunch of fashionistas fuelling up for a night at the Jazz Bar, or wherever these people went, these days. Behind them, two beardy men ate in silence.

How could she have answered him?

In front of Sarah, an over-excited young couple made no attempt to hide the fact that they had just arrived in these parts, ready to return to this round-the-clock eatery in all those nights to come, city life-drunk begging for a 3am soup, before entering the first one-bedroom flat of their lives.

How could she have simply nodded?

Peter was ready to move this relationship to another level, but Sarah was involved with something that meant more to her than anything ever had.

She had obligations to meet, a truth to live up to.

"Let me know when you have made up your mind, okay?" Peter had said as they had left Yum Yum:

No walk in the park.

No glass in their garden.

No shared celebration of life, but a sweetly worded ultimatum from someone who had no idea what the mission meant to Sarah because Sarah had never explained the mission to him properly. How could she give up everything they had achieved in there?

"I will let you know, Peter," and:

"I will."

But here she was, still.

Lost in-between, with no indication or hint or any guidance from anyone, but herself.

Sarah dipped a piece of squishy bread into her soup.

Here she was: right in the middle.

She had a bite.

Hiding inside of Somine, while up the road, there was a boyfriend, who had made it clear to her that he was only prepared to accept an answer in black or white.

While, down the road, there was Max.

While, down the road, there was a project that had changed her life in a way no one could have expected, and she couldn't just walk away from it.

Sarah sighed.

She hadn't spoken to Max since she had arranged, with a business woman's shrewd calculation, a little more breathing space, even though she had known then, already, that she was only postponing the only thing that could get her out of this terrible state, all fingernails bitten off already:

A decision.

A choice, simple and beautiful, but Sarah drifted away again and into the street's endless stream of sad faces and lonely faces and vaguely happy faces, London's edges rubbing against each other to produce the friction this city was running on.

Was that him?

Sarah looked again.

The floating masses had shied away from the threatening drone that was about to turn into movement: he crawled across the red-light junction alone.

Jonathan?

The honking didn't seem to bother him. He looked as if he needed the sleep Sarah couldn't get much more of than she did, two nights spent in a nervous sweat.

Jesus.

He looked so much worse than she could have imagined after she had seen him a few days ago, spluttering surprises outside their café.

Sarah hesitated.

Begging for the help he seemed to be needing even more desperately now than he had then.

Sarah waited.

Sarah didn't move; like a ghost, Jonathan floated through the orange that Somine's neon sign projected onto the pavement outside and was gone as suddenly as he had appeared.

Sarah shuffled on her chair.

What could she have done for him?

She shook her head.

Nothing; she would just meet him for coffee, once he had dried out from whatever it was he was pouring down his throat again, as if nothing had ever happened.

Sarah stared at the cold soup in front of her.

If only nothing had ever happened.

She pushed the plate away.

If only this was just about choosing between boyfriend, or no boyfriend.

Between Berlin, or here.

If only this was straight-forward; Sarah stared at her hands, weirdly at rest in her lap.

Unfortunately, it wasn't.

Unfortunately, the question that was re-playing in her head, again and again, wasn't what it would look like to anyone who hadn't gone through everything she had gone through since three strangers had crashed into her life in December.

Her eyes lost focus.

This was the most difficult decision Sarah had ever taken, because it went straight to the heart of her existence.

Sarah looked up again.

Absolutely everything would be effected by it.

She shuffled.

This was about keeping on the fight against the Old World, or rejoining it, and it was the biggest question Sarah had ever asked herself. She picked up the last olive and started chewing.

And chewing.

And chewing.

"Strange, isn't it? I always thought it was the other way round. Weren't you the one who fell in love with him?"

"No... well, yes," Lizzie said, and:

"I'll explain another time, okay?"

Max pushed himself up in his bed a little. The window-less, bare room that made up his share of the squat was dark apart from the artificial blue shine that came from his mobile phone.

"It's just that –"

"Why is that so hard to understand? I just have to get this finished and then..."

"And then? Listen, all I'm saying is that Jonathan needs you."

"And how do you know that?"

"How do I know? Well, he kind of told me. He's been hanging out with me, you know. He's been asking questions he shouldn't be asking."

"What does that mean?"

He had no time for this either.

There was this post to be thought over, a decade of shame. A quarter of a century of broken promises. Years of theatre by those in charge, but not a hint of the courage that was needed if they all wanted a chance to go on.

"Well, I'll explain another time," he said.

"Right."

This was the post that would return her smiles in admiration. The fuel Max was running on.

"Just promise me that you'll get in touch with him, okay?" he said, but Lizzie didn't reply.

"Just tell him that all will be good."

"Right."

"Right."

"I will, okay? I will. But that means I have to get on with it now."

She let out a little laugh and said:

"And good luck with the revolution. How's it going?"

"Can't you see that for yourself?"

Evidence on every street.

Conviction in every heart.

"I'm in Hackney Wick, forgotten? All I see is rubble. As for the real world, now, that's something else..."

"The real world, eh?"

"Anyway, I have to go. Speak soon, okay?" Lizzie said and Max nodded to himself; as soon as Sarah had returned they would beam this post out to all those that were only waiting for the final push.

"Yes, speak soon."

"And... Max?"

"What?"

"Thanks, okay?"

"Sure." The artificial blue shine that came from his mobile phone faded away slowly.

Then it was dark.

Max pulled up his blanket.

Then it was quiet.

No one else was at home.

He closed his eyes.

There was no other breathing, but his own, alone, once again, even though he was on board with a million others. Even though he was in touch with a thousand followers, he could only hear himself; Max pulled the blanket up closer.

He knew it was here again.

Max opened his eyes, but it didn't help: the nagging black demon had made it again.

He shuffled.

The fat and ugly monster that only had a chance here, outside of Café Oto's protective walls, was sitting on his chest:

All the bridges had been burnt.

Max twisted.

The grimace that only had a chance here, far away from Sarah's sweet words in support, stuck.

And it started hissing.

Max had decided what he had decided, an existence spent waiting for a life on the inside replaced by writing and walking. Replaced by a life that was hanging by a thread.

He turned.

He had decided what he had decided, becoming a radical outsider on the run, and that meant that he would never be able to lead a normal life again, all of society's accepted ambitions shunned for the daring action that was taken inside of Café Oto.

Where ambition was defined otherwise.

Max shuffled up.

He had dumped everything for this, his own way, scribbling down words as he walked the streets of Hackney, placing his battered notebook on a black rubbish bin or a dusty bonnet in order not to lose thoughts he couldn't afford to lose.

Because, by now, these thoughts were all he had.

Max had snubbed everyone.

The demon sneered.

Max had put two lives on a single card in a game that knew no jokers.

Having ditched the battle for good, there was only one way to get out of this.

He tried to breathe calmly.

He had reduced all of life's meaning to one mad idea and having leaned out of life's conventional frame as far as they had, the truth was this:

Victory was the only option.

Having come this far, the truth was that victory's glorious fanfare was around the corner.

The whole crowd in a thundering roar.

"Keep going," she had written.

Max placed his arms next to his body and concentrated on his breathing.

"Keep going."

His arms and legs were getting heavier. His blood was turning into a thick brew.

He needed the pictures.

His blood was turning into the kind of slow flow that intensified with every image that came on:

A thousand fists in the air.

A million raging shouts.

In his veins, the bubbles grew with every memory that flooded his head, the street of their city filled with anger. The anger about to boil over.

Max soaked this up, sweet proof that it was all happening.

Their message was on a million lips and everyone had only waited for someone to take the lead.

"We are doing this."

Max needed the image, her hair being unruffled slightly by an April wind as she said from behind her large sunglasses:

"We really are."

Hand in hand, delivering what would write this mission into the history books.

Hand in hand, pushing forward with a smile.

Arm in arm, onwards, because they felt what everyone around them had to feel:

That the explosion was imminent.

Jonathan banged the empty glass onto the counter and pushed his way to the front:

They could fucking have it.

This mad idea was turning a little more real with every minute that passed; he pushed the door and lit his cigarette the moment he stepped onto the pavement.

They would fucking see.

He dragged as hard as he could, but everything he did only made the precious click move further away, five bottles of Asahi in vain: his last companion had switched sides.

The click was out of reach.

He was practically dead.

Jonathan dragged again.

"You come here often?" a boyish beard beneath a black trilby asked him out of nowhere, just the way Jonathan had used to, chat by chat dragging his skinny jeans arse where Jonathan wasn't getting.

"I live here, yes."

Still playing the insider, even though he hated the Dalston Superstore for dumping Shoreditch at his doorstep, the 149 filled to the brim with the clueless fucking hordes that came up the road weekend for weekend now, expecting Disneyland.

Just because the newspapers had started saying so.

"Pretty cool area, isn't it?" the guy said, nervously tapping his feet to a non-existing beat. Moving, on a Dalston pavement, to music that was only playing inside his own head. Catching a rhythm Jonathan was so desperately trying to get back.

"You bet it is," he said.

Done this, done that.

Been everywhere; Jonathan wanted to shout at the guy that he was still here, still kicking.

He dragged.

That he was still commandeering these fucking bars just the way he used to, entire weekends without a minute of sleep.

And dragged.

That he was still ruling his beat, a lit Marlboro constantly hanging from lips formed in a trademark grin as he strode on, seducing female London with a shrug; Jonathan wanted to shout it out loud, but the guy just said:

"Alright, see you."

Just the way Jonathan had used to, a fag-length conversation used and abused. A connection cut before it became a burden, moving on, flying high.

Jonathan had another drag.

But not for him.

He flicked the butt onto the street and turned around; he couldn't let this go.

He pushed his way through the concrete cool that made this newcomer the over-crowded favourite it had become in such a short time to start begging, one more time, for reaction.

"Two Whisky Cokes, please."

Just like then, two straws each, only that this time round, they were both for him.

Because Lizzie was fucking the Wick instead.

Jonathan pushed over the money and had a large sip the moment he placed the glasses in front of him.

He turned around.

Black curls to the rescue?

He had another sip.

"What are you staring at?" she said and, before Jonathan could even think of a reply:

"Freak."

A few months. A few miles up the road: Was that all it took? Jonathan put the empty glass on the counter.

Tempted by the inside, he had left the outside behind.

For this?

Lured by a life that was cushy and tender, he had carelessly done what he should never have done, despite the sex whenever he wanted to and the waking up next to each other and the holding on tight:

He had conceded the outside to others.

"Hey," he said to a blonde girl that was waiting to be served next to him; it was all still there, wasn't it?

His eyes, doing the trick.

His legs, moving without being asked; Jonathan picked up the other drink.

His failure-proof strategy, working out exactly the way it had a hundred times before, from one fuck to the next.

It was all still there.

The bars that littered his city were ready to welcome him again and forget the slip, weren't they?

"Hey," he said again.

A hundred sticky floors were ready to forgive.

But the blonde girl just ignored him.

"Well, fuck you," he said and had another large sip; there was no point, was there?

He had crossed the line.

The legend had become a freak.

The stray dog was dead.

"Fuck you," he said again, but she didn't react. There was a wall between him and them now.

Jonathan had another sip.

The babies with bottles that had taken his space were operating on another fucking frequency and there was no way to get it all back, a postcard picture from a nobler past:

An unbroken chain of blowjobs.

A procession of ejaculations, his life lived in the glaring light of this city's convenience shops, from one bed to the next.

His orgasm parade.

It was all over, riding a never-ending wave of pints and pills to get it on with mini-skirted strangers on shabby couches and Shoreditch toilets:

"We can't fuck here, man."

"Oh really?" and:

"You see."

It was all gone, standing surrounded by a hundred lipsticked temptations in the middle of the brightly-lit dance floor that had been his life, not giving a shit what those around him thought, as he danced on and on; it was all gone:

The wave was broken.

Lizzie had robbed him of his glorious past just the way Jonathan had wanted her to, the need for another war:

Suppressed.

But now Lizzie was gone.

As was his job.

As was everything else and Max the moron had been damn right the other day.

Only that he was still wasting his time.

Only that he was still far too tame for any of this, because this life hadn't fucked him the way it had Jonathan:

The office had shut him out.

Lizzie had shut him out.

And now the Dalston fucking Superstore was shutting him out too, a hundred surely-faced toddlers sneering into his face without any regard for anything.

Treatment like that made boys cry..

Treatment like that made people like Jonathan do other things, a mad idea having just turned into a plan; he banged the empty glass onto the counter.

As if steered, once again...

Who would stop him?

Jonathan started pushing his way through the stupid grins and the fake smiles.

Who still gave a fuck what he got up to?

Jonathan elbowed himself out.

"Hey, easy, man."

"Yeah, fuck you too."

Jonathan pushed the door; the truth was: There was no one left to stop him.

Lizzie touched the outer fringes.

This was the most direct flow possible, everything she had put into her piece flowing back at her.

Lizzie let her fingers glide over the surface, tenderly touching what she had created.

The energy was tangible in every pore.

The power was in every corrugation; Lizzie's hands moved further down, where things became rougher.

Rawer.

Real; she was nearly there. She had almost reached what she had been working towards without a break, a sleeping bag in the corner, a toothbrush on the floor; everything she needed was provided from the small shop next to the station, where the ghosts that remained came for bread and hummus and new tobacco just like her.

She took a step back.

The bare light bulb that dangled from the concrete ceiling in the middle of her studio kept away the night that surrounded it. A hissing wind blew the stink of waste through the forsaken warehouse. In the far distance, a siren wailed, but all other sounds had died away.

Lizzie took a deep breath.

She had recovered from its earlier attack, but it was still there, lurking in the corner:

This nasty new question mark.

The one that was pushed aside, usually.

Lizzie shook her head.

Why was this one so much bigger than all those Lizzie had eradicated taken together?

The one that was usually ignored.

Or drowned.

In sound or booze or whatever else was available out there, but not in here; Lizzie made another step back, but it refused to go, still only waiting shamelessly to fill the precious space Lizzie had created for herself.

Was that the deal?

Having dumped the pubs, where a new crowd was sheepishly smiling as they rolled their cigarettes and ordered their pints and felt good about having received the baton from the likes of Lizzie, the lead part in a play called East London handed over to a new cast.

Having left.

Having replaced her whimsical strive for recognition in the eyes of everyone but herself with a whole new truth.

A whole new space inside her head.

Having shut out every last one of life's distraction for this self-imposed solitude, all her usual worries and doubts beaten to arrive at a blank new page.

Was this her reward?

Lizzie rubbed her eyes, but it didn't help.

It kept lurking.

It kept looking, fully prepared to jump at her again, just the way it had a little earlier, when stars had taken her sight and shudders had taken her balance:

The why at all.

Lizzie sighed.

Was that really what she had done all this for, the big one, sensing a chance for revenge?

Just because it was endlessly numbed?

Just because, out there, it was endlessly overrun by moments of semi-affection, fake moans of pleasure to silence its haunting cry, or another overpriced round.

Just because, out there, it could be dumped for another ride through this acquired homeland of illusion, bright lights, big city, but in here it stuck:

A forgotten inquest.

A puzzle that had been laid to rest a long time ago, even though the answer had never been found, childhood curiosity pushed into its place by a need to move on in a world that didn't value childhood curiosity.

A mystery no one fancied solving.

Only to catch up now?

As if it had only waited for the right moment to strike.

As if it had only waited for this, space having been cleared by Lizzie herself.

She pinched herself.

Had she really thrown all her ballast over board only to see this pest claim the space she had created?

The big one, saying hello.

The big one sensing a weakness, all guidance having been shrugged off in the name of freedom and God having been discarded as far too easy an explanation.

A convenient way out of too many situations.

A lazy answer?

Lizzie tried to calm herself down; was there a better one amid these ruins?

Was there hope amid the wreckage?

She walked over to the window.

Was there enough time to find out? What Max had told her on the phone earlier didn't want to leave.

He had sounded so serious.

He had sounded too worried about the one person that still mattered more than anyone; but what could she possibly say to Jonathan, other than that she was nearly there?

That she was almost ready to return.

Very soon, the last piece would be in place and then it wouldn't even matter what happened, her work trashed, dismissed, stolen, so what. She just had to get there and once she was, it didn't even matter if she woke up to find it all discarded a few minutes down the road from here, debunked as junk, a myth.

Utterly useless for anyone, but her.

It would be the perfect exhibition, this world's crash turned into art only to be smashed onto the street of the zone; all she would have to do was cordon off the area and print a few flyers and lean back and enjoy.

But what could she possibly say to Jonathan right now?

There wasn't even a chance that her carefully chosen words would make it through his drunkenness intact and the risk was too great, her flow disturbed forever:

If she didn't manage to bring this to a satisfactory end, everything would have been in vain.

If she didn't get there properly, all she would be left with was this nagging new question mark, nothing gained, but everything lost, and that meant that she had to keep going.

That meant that she had to keep using the enthusiasm that was left and ignore these ripples.

And ignore this temptation to break.

She sighed.

In the far distance, she could make out the red lights that topped the line-up of cranes. Coming on and off in regular intervals, they were ready to twinkle her into the satisfied sleep she had grown used to in here, but there couldn't be any sleep until she was finished. She had to get this done, before she could talk to Jonathan.

Lizzie turned around and walked towards her piece again.

She had to hurry up.

The sunshine that came through the window of her bedroom warmed Sarah's cheeks.

Slowly, she opened her eyes.

Slowly, she greeted a new day and this sunshine was stronger than any sunshine she had seen in a long time.

She squinted.

Every beam that stroked her tired face seemed to be hailing a day that felt bound to be special for reasons that weren't quite apparent yet.

Sarah stretched.

She had only fallen asleep a few hours earlier, after she had carried her heavy thoughts from Somine back to a comfort zone that had turned into a prison.

Had everything been just a dream?

Was her dilemma resolved?

Sarah pushed away the blanket; nothing was resolved. She was still lying inside her bed the way she had for days now, no input or output or anything at all.

Nothing had changed.

Peter was still at work and Max was still in their café and Sarah was still here.

Not a thing was resolved and it would stay that way until Sarah got up and acted.

She knew that.

She pushed herself up a little; there hadn't been a glow like this since last summer and last summer seemed longer ago than anything ever had.

A fading memory.

A vague idea.

A distant past that had been pushed away by a winter that had turned out worse than anything had ever been, a temptation turned into a disaster, and here she was, lying in her bed exactly the way she had then, when all of a sudden the light had come in from all sides because Sarah had opened what had never been opened.

The box: gone.

When things had happened she still only half understood.

She closed her eyes.

She knew that she shouldn't allow this, but another force was winning the argument, once again, and managed to switch on her bathroom light, Sarah's head against the tub:

No.

No.

No.

Another force was replaying her own screams to her. The screams no one had heard.

No.

No.

As the Old World had tried to wrestle her down using its strongest weapon, guilt, and had pushed her to the neatly-tiled white floor, and the only way out had presented itself in form of a small bottle, rarely used, but known to be effective.

Sarah shuddered.

How silly she must have looked to anyone who had seen her, sinking down like that.

How weak she must have seemed, giving up.

Taking weakness to a whole new level, as she had swallowed pill after pill after pill.

How ridiculous it now seemed.

How pathetic that, on the inside, she had risen, unstoppably, on the back of her own strengths, but, once outside, she had been totally unable to stand up for her choice, however mad and rushed and irrational it had been.

Squeezing the bottle in her shivery hands until it had started to get dark...

Sarah rushed up.

Were the others thinking back as often as she was? There was sweat on her forehead.

It was as if she could feel their presence.

Were they as haunted?

As if they were coming closer again...

She had to call Jonathan, the sad apparition that had hovered past Somine last night.

How empty his eyes had looked.

How tired he had seemed, capable of nothing, but ready for whatever this world would throw his way.

She had to meet him some day soon.

Sarah turned.

Perhaps she could get all four of them together again?

Perhaps there was a way...

On their bedside table, her mobile phone was ringing. She looked at the display.

She rubbed her eyes.

Nothing made her dizzier than these attacks from the past.

She pressed green.

"Hey."

"Hey."

"How are you?"

"Fine. Listen Sarah, I can't talk long, but I just heard that I can take the afternoon off. Let's meet somewhere and finally talk properly, okay?"

Sarah swallowed.

"What do you think?" Peter said.

"Yes, sure, that'd be great. Where shall we meet?"

"Why don't you come my way and we go for coffee somewhere around here?"

How she was missing making plans like that, calling from work to arrange a shared bottle of wine or a film or a dinner close to either of their offices. How it all reminded her of their early days, having just moved in:

A future, but shared.

"Yes, sure," Sarah said, and:

"Sure. See you then."

She pressed red; when this world had been their playground and this flat their base, busy weeks followed by lazy Saturdays and whole Sundays spent inside. When this city had been their city and this their bed. Where sex hadn't happened in weeks now.

Sarah sunk down again.

How she missed those feelings, de-activated by thoughts that refused to stay outside their door, another worry about a bigger picture that had no respect for the fact that there was a smaller picture to be considered as well. Her hands moved down her body. How she missed these desires, switched off by another meaningless argument, just because Sarah had adjusted her priorities and the switch hadn't worked.

Could she get it all back?

The intensity that, for a short while, had made it seem like Peter and she were the only people in this city, their city, London: home.

This city, their city.

Which was far too diverse to be categorised, labelled, tagged: Unlike most cities, London couldn't be described, because the moment you tried, a new impression came along, rebutting everything.

Teaching you a lesson.

Which meant that you made your own city and they had: Peter and her.

Sarah sighed.

But Max needed her. She had committed herself to a mission that had given her everything she had missed for such a long time and there was so much left to do:

A whole future remained in their hands.

There was so much that had to be finished and she couldn't just drop this, could she?

She couldn't just give it up.

Max had asked her over and over again if she was absolutely sure that she wanted to go ahead and she had said:

"Yes," and:

"Yes," and:

"Absolutely."

Sarah had signed up and told herself over and over again that the running away had stopped. That the shying away had ended that night in December, but all this hardly helped:

Peter's mind was made up.

He had been given the opportunity of his life and followed the mantra they had laid out for each other a long time ago, but wasn't the mission Sarah's career now?

She turned around.

She had to get up and get ready and see Peter and tell him where she was coming down.

Between giving up half-away, and losing him forever.

Between going forward, or turning around.

Between staying where she was, or returning to an inside that was getting brighter again; it was one world or the other now, there was no talking around that.

Harmony was no longer an option.

Another compromise wasn't on and she had less than two hours; the ripples created by her journey into the past were being replaced by the terrible itch that had ruled her body for far too many days now.

It seized her from top to bottom.

There was no talking around it any longer. Sarah pushed away the blanket and got up.

Was this slipping?

London Fields had started the party, bottles of red wine being passed beneath its towering planes.

Was this a sign?

Another gang on a blanket was turning up the stereo, but Max kept walking, quickly, through the heady mix of freshly-lit barbecues and re-lit spliffs. All around him, careful smiles were pushing away the worries that had provided him with his fire:

Was this sliding out of hand?

Max had heard too much in the last few hours.

About the worst being over.

About things having started to return to normal again, green shoots having been sighted by those inclined to use idiotic metaphors like that.

As if green shoots could grow on rubble.

Max shook his head.

He had read too much about all being half as bad and about a hundred causes for optimism and a generous permission from all those still clinging to all those still fretting to finally let go.

And forget.

And return; Max stepped over someone's legs only to be cut short by a Labrador in blind pursuit of a tennis ball, roars of applause as he crashed through a pile of empty cans.

Max had seen enough.

Mischievous attempts to derail their success were sprouting up all around him and there was only one way to react and that was a post to beat all posts, the bomb he still hadn't managed to write. Because this crack wasn't going away.

He needed her.

Max passed dresses that had much more trust in this early sunshine than appropriate, whole armies of potential followers hidden behind fake Ray Bans in red and white and green. He kicked back a football that came flying straight at him just as his mobile announced a text message:

His partner, finally?

He stopped next to a disposable grill that hosted fat Cumberland sausages next to sizzling slices of halloumi. The dreadlocked guy in charge of operations cracked another can into spreading its foaming temptation for more.

And more.

And more.

"Fireworks at 12. Look south for the show."

Max read it again.

What the hell was that supposed to mean?

He put the mobile back into his pocket and started walking again; what was Jonathan trying to tell him?

Max stepped from the grass onto the pathway, where bikes were beating prams as a grinning loner provided a deranged running commentary for no one but himself through his toothless, uncontrolled mouth.

"We have to stop the slipping," Max mumbled, solidarity in soliloquizing.

"We have to act."

But these words were all he had come up with so far: another clumsy draft that lacked all the poetry and elegance and wit and power that had turned his early posts into such crackers. He had deleted every word this morning. He had erased a whole page, just like that. Just because he didn't get the nod he needed.

Max took out his mobile and fired off the same text message he had sent three times already:

"Hey Sarah. Any news?"

He kept the phone in his hand.

The mission had to be stepped up before these sunbeams could destroy everything.

The risk was all around Max.

The fear that had shaken them all to the bone: swallowed with another Becks.

All the gloom and all the doom: puffed away.

The inconvenient truth that came out of Café Oto, conveniently absorbed in the smoke of these barbecues, feather-like floating towards this beautiful sky in blue.

Where no one cared for them either.

In front of Max, The Pub on the Park was doing its best to keep the illusion alive, pint by pint, convincing everyone in line for escapism on tap that it had all been a blip, no more:

No need to worry.

No need to sweat.

Max shook his head; he wanted to shout at them: that the clocks were still ticking.

That this was still the abyss, blue sky or not.

That it was all still there.

But Max had to reserve his anger for a blank new page, a brand new piece. He had to wait until he had returned to his table, the only place he belonged; he had to wait until the crack was gone.

Above him, the trees rustled, eyes closed, as if they were the sea.

Max twitched.

Finally?

He looked at the mobile in his hand.

"Hi Max, I will call you in an hour okay? xx"

He smiled.

That was it, wasn't it?

Yes!

He turned left again and started striding, without a second of hesitation, straight towards his screen, with shirts and skirts and sunshades all turning into one bright stream of colour that no longer bothered him at all.

Yes!

He smiled and smiled.

This was it.

"If we let this slip out of our hands now, friends, we will not only have to look into the eyes of our children, accusing us of having made their life hell, we will also have to look into the mirror every morning and justify why, knowing everything we knew, why, friends, we did nothing while we still could."

It came out in one flow.

"Shrugging off the best chance we would ever get to redesign everything because the sun was out."

Max punched the air.

He started running towards this piece, forming in front of his eyes, word for word.

Sentence for sentence.

Yes!

He jumped over lame bodies and children's bikes and cooling boxes, his sleep-deprived body on a level of energy that had seemed all but impossible a few minutes ago.

This was it.

It was all there; he would knock this out in no time. Max sped up even more.

He would be ready when she called.

He would be holding the bomb they had been waiting for in his hands, her eyes glowing with admiration.

Max jumped.

He would be ready to proclaim that the grand finale was around the corner:

The countdown could start.

Lizzie lowered her arm.

A whole night spent whirling through her studio like a possessed witch had just brought her to the end. The last piece was in place. Her right arm kept sinking alongside her body and joined the other one, hanging loose:

She had arrived.

There was no question about it; around her, the sound of the diggers faded away. The bulldozers that had provided the comforting backdrop to her Great Project seemed to be driving off.

Everything calmed down.

Lizzie tried to focus, but her eyes told her otherwise. In front of her, the piece started to blur:

There were no more shapes.

There were no more edges.

There was no friction left at all; Lizzie took a few steps backwards. What was this?

Crawling up inside of her...

As if someone had just taken all the weight of the world from her exhausted shoulders.

Lizzie took another step backwards and started sinking onto the chair behind her.

As if someone had just sucked away the last remaining tension.

She put her hands in her lap.

So content, finally.

And so still; her own breathing was the only sound that still filled the cold, bare room that surrounded her:

This was her own achievement.

This was the journey's end.

Her eyelids started gliding down and the blur made way for nothing at all:

This was absolute peace, taking over.

Her mind was turning into an endless white desert, where nothing else existed, but this warm and mellow calm.

Where a weak wind was blowing the sand, just a little, before it started slowing down, further and further, until the sand had settled down completely and everything stood still; Lizzie ripped open her eyes and jumped up.

What the fuck was happening?

The chair tipped over behind her, but the sound it made arrived as a mere thud.

Everything turned.

Lizzie closed her eyes again, but it was still there, stretching in white.

Lizzie opened her eyes again.

Had she gone too far?

She started sinking down, slowly; had she crossed a border she hadn't even seen?

Her right hand stretched out to grab the open pack of Golden Virginia that was lying in front of her. She pulled it close and grabbed a bunch of tobacco. Her shivery hands started rolling, but half the tobacco fell out again; was this her reward?

She licked.

The clacking of her lighter hardly registered and neither did the crackling of her first drag.

Her mind was a blank.

She dragged again; the murderous question mark was still there and this white desert left Lizzie without a defence.

She exhaled through her nose.

The wicked newcomer was still lurking, ready to jump at her any minute and fill this daunting new space with its unbearable pervasiveness, its terrible ability to touch things inside of her that shouldn't be touched: Lizzie was too close to the fucking essence.

Lizzie was too close to the core.

She rushed up.

There was no other way, was there? She grabbed her bag and rushed to the door; the weird calm she had created inside her body, an unknown contentment flowing through all her veins, was inviting things she didn't know how to handle and there was no alternative, but to escape, down the piss-stained, rubbish-strewn staircase and onto the street.

Where the debris still spread.

Where the pieces still lay.

Lizzie started running.

Away from the splinters. Away from the stink. Away from a studio that had liberated her from absolutely everything only to turn into a completely new kind of a cage, all four walls moving in on her at the same time.

Had that really been the idea?

She ran and ran.

Away from the broken glass. Away from the mud. Away from the toxic dust that whirled through the air everywhere. The forsaken warehouses that followed her left and right seemed to laugh at her.

Hollow sneers seemed to come from every black hole:

The Wick was closing in.

"Fuck."

The Wick was threatening to swallow her up in her self-imposed solitude and if she wanted a chance to get away, she needed voices that didn't come out of her own mouth.

If she wanted to survive, she needed cars and crowds, crescendo.

Lizzie tripped.

If she wanted to go on, she needed life.

Lizzie caught herself; she could almost see the bridge that would return her to the real Hackney, sirens hunting down Stoke Newington High Street and Mare Street buzzing with a hundred different languages.

How she was looking forward to it all.

Preacher men singing their prophesies to Kingsland Road pavements and her crew's laughs echoing through Broadway Market again, the whole street scented by daytime drinking's aftertaste.

How she was looking forward to the whole soothing show, leaning against the counter of The George again to breathe its infatuating perfume and order another Whisky Coke for every familiar face she could gather around her, nicely filling this space, once again.

Before something else would.

Lizzie stopped.

How could she not have noticed this warmth earlier?

She looked up.

A glorious sunshine was coming down at the terrain that lay on the other side of the border.

A shy smile started taking over her face.

A beautiful day was taking place in the land she called home and how she was looking forward to diving into it, cold Cider being bought from convenience shops for the first time this year and loved-up couples lying beneath the trees in London Fields. How she was looking forward to falling into the arms of someone she should have called much, much earlier.

"God, Sarah, in some ways you're still as naïve as you were when you met that guy for the first time," Peter said.

"What do you mean?"

Sarah hugged her cup of coffee just the way Max had hugged his when they had first met, in another café, at a different time. In another world.

Peter leaned over the table and looked her into the eyes.

"Do you really think everyone said that it was a good idea to join Max and his nonsense because they believed it?"

"Why else would they have?"

Everyone had nodded.

Everyone had told her that it was at least worth a try.

He shock his head.

"It was just that, you know... after..."

He looked into his cup, still not able to approach the great taboo. The picture that was best forgotten.

Sarah nodded.

"It was just that, afterwards, everyone was scared to touch you, Sarah. Everyone... We... We were all afraid to be to harsh to you... to do something wrong, you know?"

"What?"

"I was..."

"What? And that was the reason all of you encouraged me to join Max, is that what you're saying?"

"Well, no one exactly encouraged you, but, yes... That was the reason we kept back some of our, you know, reservations."

This was ridiculous.

Peter moved the spoon around in his cup without any apparent purpose. The nondescript, business-like café he had chosen, the Old World screaming from every wall, was becoming more of a torture chamber with every sentence that was being spoken.

Did Peter really mean what he was saying?

"We just thought we should see what would happen and give you some more time to find yourself again and..."

He stared at her.

"I mean, no one expected you to jump in there the way you did and... and forget everything else."

He looked down.

"And forget me."

"I haven't forgotten you, Peter!"

She almost screamed this.

She had signed up in the firm belief that the mission had been the only move that had made any sense after December's crash had ended the party everyone had so light-heartedly enjoyed all those years, without ever thinking about the day after. Without ever thinking at all. She had joined Max convinced that the hangover had left them no choice.

Convinced that everyone had agreed.

"I would never forget you," she said and took his hand.

"Well," he said, and:

"It's not too late. It's all in your hands. It's your choice. You know what my plans are. You have to make yours. I mean, no one traps you in that café. No one traps you anywhere."

Sarah nodded.

Peter got up.

"I'm just going to the toilet, okay?"

She nodded.

And kept nodding as Peter walked through business meeting and lunchtime affairs.

The words kept re-playing in Sarah's head:

"It's your choice."

She moved her cup.

Forward.

And back.

Peter was right.

What if she hadn't twitched, last minute, to press three numbers on her mobile?

What if good fortune hadn't been on her side the way it had, for reasons that were only known to whoever was in charge of good fortune?

What if it all had ended differently?

She moved her cup.

Forward.

And back.

But it hadn't. That was the point. She had woken, still alive, in a bed on the second floor.

Where they were used to dealing with wounded bodies and, sometimes, wounded souls.

Where three pale faces had stared at her in disbelief.

Where she had learnt a lesson no one but herself would ever fully understand and she had acted with the best of intentions afterwards, hadn't she?

Staying true to herself for the first time ever.

She had decided what she had decided and she didn't blame Max for anything.

Sarah let go off her cup.

And still.

She shook her head.

This was laughable, getting tortured, once again, by a question that had entered her head for the first time in another café, at a different time, the inside and the outside pitching themselves against each other in the most brutal fashion.

"It's your choice."

It all came down to the same base, only that, this time, she wouldn't be able to escape to the neatly-tiled, cold white floor of her bathroom, because you only had that joker once.

Only that, this time, there was no exit sign.

Sarah leaned back.

And whoever was hanging out up there was unprepared to step in and lift her burden.

Whatever was hanging out up there kept its mouth shut, just the way it was constantly ordered.

Sarah saw her mobile flashing up on the table in front of her, the apparition with a text:

"Thanks for not being there for me."

Shit.

"But never mind."

Shit.

"See you for the fireworks."

What?

What the hell was that supposed to mean?

Oh, Jonathan.

The display went black again, just as Peter appeared at the end of the room and started walking towards her with a strong, attractive determination she had lost along the way; they could make love all night, couldn't they?

They could make babies and simply forget the rest, Max and the mission.

Couldn't they?

They could hold on to each other forever and remind themselves that, if this world was really coming to an end, there was only one thing that counted anyway.

Peter took his seat opposite her again.

That, if it was really all true, there was only one thing that mattered anyway.

And that was love.

She looked at him, but he didn't say anything. His face wasn't angry or worried or strange at all. He didn't look pushy and he didn't look mad; he just smiled at her, warm and caring and sweet. And Sarah took his hand and tried to smile the same way back at him.

Victory, oh, victory!

Not even helicopters were getting the picture now. The entire city was a sea of fists and flags.

Oh, glorious success, every office abandoned, all streets jammed. The entire city was up in arms.

Street for street, the fired-up masses were singing their song of a world, where life was no longer lived on the back of a burning planet, but in harmony with it.

Where a short-term madness for the benefit of the few had finally been replaced by a fresh perspective, respecting all.

Where everyone got the chance to contribute to making this life more liveable still.

Oh, victory!

Joining their hands as human beings, a scattered society was coming together, once and for all, and leading the millions was Max, chin-raised striding, his vision in his eyes. His determination written all over his face.

And next to Max was Sarah.

Together they had delivered the spell everyone had only waited for and, right now, they were reaping the benefit, proudly leading a parade that would change everything forever.

They looked at each other.

"I love you," Sarah said to him.

Her arms were slung around his waist as they kissed; a long and intimate kiss, totally unperturbed by the shuffling that was going on around them.

"And I love you more than anything," Max said.

And then they took each other's hand and started looking south for the fireworks; Max jerked up his head.

Jesus.

He was covered in sweat. He rubbed his left cheek, covered in furrows from the keyboard.

South for the fireworks?

Jesus.

He pushed back the chair he was sitting on; was it too late? His eyes were still glued together.

Jesus, Jonathan.

Could he be serious?

Max looked at his watch: he had ten minutes; could Jonathan really have taken on board everything he had told him to pervert it like that?

Max grabbed the mobile that was lying next to his screen.

Could he fucking mean this?

He dialled his number as he grabbed his jumper only to drop his jumper again; no answer.

"Shit, shit, shit."

Max rushed around the table and gestured at the girl behind the bar to keep an eye on his computer, just the way he had done a hundred times.

Jesus, Jonathan.

How could he have not realised much earlier what he had tried to tell him.

Max pushed the door.

This couldn't be true; he dialled the number again as he rushed down Aswhin Street, but there was no answer: There was no other way, but to get there before Jonathan, but south wasn't exactly an accurate description, was it?

Max started running alongside the construction site walls that lined Dalston Lane, stepping left and right to make way for strangers who had no idea what kind of shit was about to go down.

The 149 was speeding down the High Street as he reached the junction, red lights in his way.

"Fuck."

This was his only chance; he clutched his phone and sprinted, honk-hit, between cars and past the corner Chinese he had never been to, but all he saw was this bus, spitting out aliens, picking up aliens.

About to speed off.

"Wait," Max shouted, knowing all too well that it wouldn't change a thing.

"Fucking wait!"

He almost pushed an old man onto the street, shouts of half-felt outrage from all sides, before dashing his shoulder against a pram-pushing mum, who started screaming abuse that didn't reach him anymore in his final sprint, all energy summoned, to jump, without weighing the consequences:

Another trademark leap of faith.

Another ridiculous gamble.

His shoes were gliding off, but his shoulders got squeezed by the closing doors, beep, beep, beep; they bucked and retreated and Max almost fell back onto the street, but he grabbed whatever arm he could grab to pull himself in, mumbles of amusement and a whole bus looking at his red head as the doors closed again, beep, beep, beep, and the bus started rolling, as if this was normal procedure:

"149. To: London Bridge."

Max grabbed a grey strap and tried to regain his breath. He was still clutching his mobile phone.

"Please pick it up," he said.

"Please, please, please."

But Jonathan didn't; Max lowered the phone from his ear and stared at the sweat-covered display.

"For fuck's sake, man."

The display lit up again.

Damn it.

What had been meant to trigger nothing but joy, brought only horror now: How was he meant to explain to Sarah that Jonathan was about to twist their belief into action that had the potential to destroy everything?

Damn it.

"Hey Sarah," he said, as calmly as possible.

"God, are you okay?"

"Yeah, I'm good... It's just... I'm on the 149, it's a bit noisy here, you know what I mean."

"Okay, perhaps I'll call later..."

"No, we can talk."

Because hearing her voice was almost enough to make the rest disappear.

"Well, it's not exactly good news and I thought –"

"What do you mean?"

"I wanted to tell you in person, it's... but there's no time. But... I think I'll call back later."

"What is it Sarah?"

"I think I have to leave."

"What do you mean, leave?"

"I mean leave. I have to go. I'm leaving London. I'm sorry Max, but I can't go on like this. It's... I have talked to Peter and we have so many plans. He has this amazing job offer in Berlin and, you know, I want kids at some point. I – it's just... You know how much I believe in the mission, but I have to do this. Do you understand?"

But Max hung up.

It just happened. There wasn't anything he could have said, feelings so mixed they cancelled each other out.

Total overflow.

The display came on again.

Damn it.

"Why did you hang up?" Sarah said, and:

"That's not fair."

"Not fair? What's not fair? You leaving me, just like that – that's not fair. Kicking our dream with two feet."

"Max."

"Why are you as fucking inconsistent as everyone else out there? Do you have an idea what you're doing?"

"Max."

"Everything we created in the last few months."

"What we created was great. We can be very proud – you can. But it kind of feels like it's over. The world is moving on, Max."

"Jesus, you're just like them."

"So it feels like the right time for me to move on too –"

"Well, fuck off then," he shouted, and:

"Kick it into the bin. Dump it all. Everything was about to start, Sarah. Millions were on our side."

"Max."

"Thousands were listening to what we had to say, but you just fuck off."

"Max."

"What?"

"There were never thousands listening."

How could she ditch everything they had achieved?

"Most of the time there weren't even hundreds reading what we put out there."

How could she walk away like that?

"Sometimes there were only a few dozen –"

"What are you talking about?"

"I'm talking about our clicks, the audience."

"Yes, they were fantastic."

"No, Max. They were never as fantastic as I said they were. I'm so sorry. I just wanted the best for you. For us. I exaggerated them. I made them up, Max, it was a nice project, the mission, but now it's time to move on, don't you understand?"

Her words and the chatter that surrounded him and the continuous honks of a truck and a procession of police cars speeding past and a crying baby next to him all became one deafening roar that dizzied him.

"Max?"

That strangled him.

"Max, are you still there?"

Victory, oh, victory!

Street after street, the picture couldn't be clearer. Street after street, the picture was real, wasn't it?

Oh, victory!

"Max, I'm going to hang up now. Are you still there? Why aren't you saying anything, Max?"

Lizzie turned right where the Truman Brewery's car-free car park hit the uneven surface of Hanbury Street and started smiling, very carefully:

The bridge had done the trick, hadn't it?

It was done!

Lizzie had dropped the nasty new question mark onto a thundering A12, where a hundred cars and trucks had ruthlessly flattened it. Conveniently making sure that it wouldn't get up for a long, long time.

Lizzie squinted into the sun.

The bridge had taken it!

The nasty new question mark was gone and this was beautiful, another long-gone summer coming back to her, sitting cross-legged on the warm concrete she had just crossed.

Raising their Red Stripes as aspiring songwriters had shared their pipedreams and everyone had shared a pack of tobacco and no one had felt the need to share a worry about anything at all. Nicely sheltered by another hat from Beyond Retro, where half an hour of browsing had, once again, taken a whole morning.

Lizzie kept smiling.

The bridge had done it, hadn't it?

Step for step Lizzie had taken across the grey concrete, the white desert, that had threatened her inside her studio, had made way for the colours she knew and the feeling of sheer relief that had come with it, had only hastened her run, hands guided by the metal railings:

Towards real life.

She had won.

Lizzie couldn't stop smiling; it wouldn't change a thing now if someone took the big metal plank and smashed her piece into a thousand tiny bits.

She was here.

She had made it, through Victoria Park and alongside the canal, leaving the water just in time to avoid December's crime scene and allow Bethnal Green to deliver happier memories:

Gallery-hopping along Vyner Street, only to end up, as if by default, in The Victory.

Ordering Stella after Stella, until dusk would suggest a new location.

Finishing off another house party in a former warehouse off Bethnal Green Road on a rooftop at dawn, chanting life, sweet life, at the early trains in the distance and the glittering Gherkin and everyone that had already been walking the streets below.

Lizzie crossed Hanbury Street.

How these memories had the power to take over completely, biting into a warm prawn roll on a hung-over Sunday morning, shade-protected wearing their lifestyle on their sleeves as they had stumbled amid the flowers of Columbia Road Market.

Rummaging through the Mile End Thrift Store on a Thursday night, only to take home the only item from its treasure-lined racks that she really hadn't needed.

Selling her self-made jewellery on Brick Lane to make just enough money for the obligatory round of drinks at The Golden Heart afterwards...

Oh, The Golden Heart.

Lizzie stopped in front of the pub and had a glimpse through the open door.

The small dog looked back at her as if it wanted to ask where she had been all those months.

How, on earth, she had managed without those Thursday night lock-ins and Friday night kick-outs.

What she had done on all those afternoons she used to spend smoking on this very pavement, watching the Liverpool Street crowds flood the latest incarnation of an area that had been rough not just around the edges as Lizzie had first set foot there...

Oh, sweetest memory.

Spending whole days inside Coffee@, where the transgender beauties had lazed next to the bagel shop geezers and Lizzie and her comrades in mad fashion, had laughed at baby-faced newcomers holding their brand new A-Z's:

Welcome to the madhouse.

Lizzie took a step towards The Golden Heart's door.

It was probably a new generation that was drinking in there now, but generation was a word like shit:

Millions lumped together by marketing jerks.

Millions thrown into a basket without any common ground by line drawers, wall erectors, prison guards, just so people like Max could lose themselves in fanciful generalisations.

Ha!

Did these people share any of her experiences?

No.

Lizzie hesitated.

She could just walk to the counter and raise her glass to having achieved something no one would ever be able to take away from her again, couldn't she?

The Wick filtering through in all its significance.

Lizzie forced herself to keep walking. She had to get hold of Jonathan first.

She wanted to celebrate this with him.

Lizzie passed the small second hand shop she had worked at before the hair salon had offered her better conditions, shampoo wounds not taken into account, only to get dumped for her Great Project, a little financial help from her parents stretched all the way here:

Absolute peace had given way to a reassuring muddle, but something told Lizzie that the low-key wrestling that was still going on behind these London remembrances was only the last step towards... what exactly?

Having left the ruins for her city again, it would take some time to get used to the place she was now inhabiting...

Was her customary swinging from one extreme to the next really eyeing an unknown middle position, the inside and the outside ready to make a deal?

"This is weird shit," she said to herself, because life was still like that, wasn't it?

You chose.

But Lizzie was choosing something else now. A world in black and white was being replaced with a compromise, of sorts, her extremist past left in a realisation that either or wasn't the only option out there.

That there was an in-between?

She took out her mobile, but there was still no sign.

She dialled.

How she missed Turkish pide for breakfast and sex for lunch and how she was looking forward to another destination-less walk through their streets, arriving in Hackney Downs just in time to see the lights come on around them, a million other existences doing their best to make up this city.

And that, whatever happened next, would always be her city, right?

That, whatever was to happen next, would always remain the only place in this world, where Lizzie could function.

Right?

He picked up.

"Hey Max, have you heard from Jonathan?"

But there was no answer.

"Max?"

Nothing.

"Hello?"

"Why don't you get your spoilt little arse to Bishopsgate for a chance to see for yourself?"

"Excuse me?" she said, and:

"Bishopsgate?"

"Where are you?"

"I'm on Commercial Street, why... I'm—"

"Well, just look up then, Lizzie," he said, and:

"Just look up."

And Lizzie looked up and Lizzie saw a cloud that was darker than any of the supposedly dark clouds she had been going on about to herself for so long, and she looked down again and she saw that the police had cordoned off Brushfield Street and she had no idea what all this was supposed to mean.

Sarah kept walking, with her eyes towards the pavement, from Old Street through Shoreditch, along Great Eastern Street, towards where exactly?

That hadn't been the idea, Max hanging up on her in anger, not a hint of what she had hoped for.

She kept looking down.

The only piece of information she had about him was the 149. Walking away from her meeting with Peter, the only plan she had come up with to catch a partner she was leaving behind with a heavy heart was a bus stop at the end of this street, his destination unknown.

But her mind was made up.

Her whole body still felt the repercussions from a kiss that had been longer than any kiss she could remember, her decision celebrated across a café table, as Sarah had watched the painful gap between them vanish and both of them move closer. And closer...

"Excuse me!"

But she wanted another minute; she needed a final chance to explain herself.

She needed a last goodbye.

"Excuse me!"

Sarah looked up.

"This road is closed, I'm afraid," the police officer in front of her said, a strange seriousness in between a dark blue and a glaring yellow.

Sarah just nodded.

"I see, okay," she said and looked up behind him and looked down hastily and stared at him and said:

"Oh. My. God."

And said:

"What happened?"

The junction where Great Eastern Street became Commercial Street was a sea of flashing blue.

She swallowed.

"There has been some sort of attack."

"Attack?"

He nodded.

"What..."

She shuddered.

"What... what kind of attack?"

"We can't talk about it yet and you can't be here. I must ask you to walk up that way."

She stared at him.

"Was it..."

She shuddered.

"Was it some kind..."

"As I said, I can't talk about it and you have to leave, please."

Was it what neither of them had ever dared to utter?

Sarah froze.

Was it the mission?

Was it?

"Was it?"

"Please, you have to leave now, please."

She kept staring at him.

"Madam!"

She turned around, as if in trance, and started walking, slowly, at first, but then swifter.

And swifter.

Was this her partner, gone mad?

And swifter.

Was this Max, unable to stomach the bitter fact that words, even if they were potentially available to millions, could only go so far?

She shook her head.

Was this his answer?

A huge crowd seamed Shoreditch High Street; he couldn't have done anything like that.

That wasn't him.

Or was it?

Hundreds of people were gazing at the black cloud of smoke at Sarah's back. This was exactly the kind of crowd they had fantasised about in Café Oto, again and again, talking themselves into a frenzy of potential and possibility, but these people weren't here to act in the name of their mission.

These people were here to see the mission go up in flames.

Sarah shook her head.

No.

Whatever had happened behind that police tape, Max couldn't have done it.

That wasn't him.

Sarah swallowed.

Or was it?

In any case, this wasn't her.

She swallowed again.

Whatever had happened behind that police tape, she had nothing to do with it.

She pushed away a hundred accusing looks, evaded a thousand silent chants.

She had no part in this, did she?

Sarah shook her head.

At her back, this story was seeing its ridiculous undertones getting blown up into unknown proportions, and she was only here, because she had allowed three strangers to enter, one after the other, and had watched as they had torn up the script of how you were supposed to meet people, tried and tested, in front of her routine-driven eyes.

She was only here because she had permitted three strangers to break all the conventions and make her desire things she had never been meant to desire and she could feel them right now, just the way she used to...

But Sarah was letting go first.

Because someone had to; the crowd started to thin out where Bethnal Green Road joined Shoreditch High Street. From the T-building onwards, this was a normal street again, London still London: people moved without any regard for each other and no one noticed Sarah as she stopped.

Everything she had been thinking in the last few hours seemed underlined, all of sudden.

Every word of her decision seemed to appear in bold.

Every letter screamed at her.

The surreal scene she was leaving behind was the missing exclamation mark to her declaration and in front of her it was almost visible now:

The road home.

She rubbed her eyes; whatever was happening at her back, this was the stretch that would lead Sarah where Sarah belonged and at the road's end, in the far distance, she could almost make them out.

They were looking back at her.

Just the way they had used to.

At the road's end, in the far distance, they were standing in line.

Just the way they had used to:

Gun in hand.

Sarah loosened; at the road's end, the soldiers were waiting for her, but they didn't look threatening at all, but almost friendly, and after all those nights and days spent inside her bed, fretting herself into a state of panic about which signals to follow and which ones to ignore, this couldn't be mistaken:

They were greeting her.

And, right now, Sarah wanted nothing more than being greeted.

After too many failed attempts of communication, this one couldn't be misunderstood:

They were calling her.

And, right now, Sarah wanted nothing more than being called.

She started smiling:

She was ready to return into the arms of those that couldn't wait to protect her again. And at the road's end, in the far distance, the soldiers started smiling back at her.

Max walked in-between a row of fire trucks. He let his right hand slide past the truck's cold steel and the uneven plastic of its grey roll-top.

Here he was, having swapped one battle for another. Only to lose that one as well?

His fingers glided over the small notch that announced the truck's front door and the fender underneath and the crude plastic that wrapped the indicator. He leaned against the truck's bonnet, still warm from its drive here; his shirt was soaked in sweat from the run. Max lowered his arms, slowly, until they were sagging from both sides of his exhausted body and stared ahead:

This was it, then.

The mini cab office and the Syrian kebab and The Light Bar had all been evacuated. The whole stretch between here and Liverpool Street Station was deserted. Everyone had fled the area so they could roll in and smack it into everyone's face, their final battleground.

Max shook his head.

Around him, a spring breeze made the ashes dance up and down and up again.

Up and down and up again.

"Excuse me!"

Up...

"Hell-o!"

...and down; the fluorescent yellow stripes on the fire-fighter's uniform twinkled in the sunlight.

Max stared at them.

"What the hell are you doing here?"

Max looked at him.

Max waited.

Max said:

"I'm watching... the result."

Four souls, having collided.

"What?"

"Nothing. I'm doing nothing here... Have people been hurt?"

"Get the hell out of here."

"I will leave immediately, I promise. Just tell me if anyone's been hurt, please."

The fire-fighter pointed at an ambulance that was parked further down the empty road, its blue lights flashing. A single person was lying on a stretcher. A medic was fixing something to his face.

"No one apart from that clown over there."

He shook his head.

Max didn't say anything.

"Whatever this joker wanted to achieve, he picked a building that was still pretty much unoccupied."

"Yes."

"Tried to burn down this glass and steel friend with a bit of petrol, our would-be-terrorist. Pretty amateurish, if you ask me. Anyway, you have to go now."

"That's because he's not a terrorist."

"Excuse me?"

"Just an immature victim of what we call modern life."

The fire-fighter looked at him.

"Are you saying that you know this lunatic?"

"Know him?"

Max started shaking his head, slowly, as he stared in the general direction of the ambulance. It was leaving him, there was no doubt about it.

He had no control:

"No, sir, I don't know him."

His eyes lost focus.

Then Max said:

"He's just a stranger."

There was nothing he could do; he pushed himself off the bonnet.

"And now, I'd better leave."

He started walking.

"I'll turn into that small pathway over there, okay? I'm glad no one has been hurt," he said, and:

"I'm very glad."

But the fire-fighter had already lowered his visor to keep fighting the mess they had created, all four of them with their unique contribution; all around Max, fire-fighters were spending time that was meant for fighting real emergencies to engage in this pathetic theatre, a bit of petrol because things hadn't quite worked out.

Max started walking towards the ambulance.

A girl in green leggings was now standing next to the medic, but she didn't seem to understand a word he said to her. Jonathan was ready to be pushed inside now. She looked up and saw Max and looked at him and there was a terrible helplessness in her eyes, but Max didn't look back at her: he kept walking, without taking another look at their scene.

He had had enough.

He kept walking past the ambulance, its blue lights flashing, and alongside the red brick wall that lined the pavement and turned into the small pathway he had mentioned to the fire-fighter; he left it all behind, Jonathan on the stretcher and Lizzie next to him. Sarah had slipped out of his hands. The mobile was lying in the gutter up the road.

As had the mission.

But, somehow, all of that was far too big to really touch him any longer.

Max walked away.

The smell of the smoke that was hanging over Bishopsgate was getting less with very step he took...

For a moment, it really had seemed as if everything could have been changed, hadn't it?

For a moment, it really had seemed as if this had been a unique chance.

For just a moment.

For just a tick.

Or had Max really been the only one who had sensed the unlikely prospect of everyone coming together?

He put his hands in his pockets.

Had he really been the only one who had felt the ecstasy of knowing that, for the first time in his life, others had cared, too? That, after all, this wasn't, everyone:

Alone.

Around him, the narrow streets of Spitalfields started spinning.

Had he really been the only who had believed the most beautiful lie?

He kept walking.

Everything he had thought and written and done was gone because no one had listened and nothing had happened and nothing ever would happen unless someone else took this up where Max had left it.

And would someone be mad enough to do that?

Having seen all this.

Who would be mad enough to imitate Max and his dangerous refusal to accept life's most basic realities, the silliness of waiting replaced with a daring go at creating a better future, only to end up with nowhere else to go?

Max took his hands out of his pockets.

Max looked around.

No one was watching him as he grabbed all that had come to him the moment he had walked out of the hospital, drunk on life, into a whole new dawn, and smashed it to the ground using all the strength he had left: A call to arms that had never required any arms, merely a little courage. No one saw him mumbling the words he had used then, so proud and confident:

"We can always try."

Max looked at the remains on the ground in front of him and mumbled:

"It's always worth trying."

He raised his arms into the air; who out there would be mad enough to pick this up?

They pushed Jonathan inside before Lizzie could say a word. The stretcher's legs gave way and that was it, not a word from either of their lips.

Not a chance for:

"Why, oh, why?"

One of the medics climbed in after Jonathan and his colleague closed the doors with two swift moves, clack, clack, and that was it, and Lizzie hadn't known what to say to either of them after they had explained what had happened in a few gruff sentences.

Not even:

"Where are you bringing him?"

Not even:

"Sorry."

The second medic climbed into the driver's cabin and closed his door and shuffled, ready to take away the need for Lizzie to articulate feelings she didn't even come close to understanding. The input she was receiving from this street was only partly successful in pushing away the miracle that had started the moment she had left the Wick behind, the inside and the outside shaking hands?

The agreement had been struck.

The desired deal had been reached somewhere between The Golden Heart and here, but it would take hours to process that new state and it didn't help that the real world was handing her this giddy overdose, the one she had ignored for too long, ready to be driven and dropped where they looked after whatever injuries he was suffering from.

Had he even seen her?

The siren had a few hiccups, before it howled into the all-too-familiar sound that had provided a thousand backdrops without meaning, because, until now, it had never howled for someone that had mattered.

But this was about Jonathan.

This had to mean something, but the hollow words that danced, as if on speed, through her overworked mind didn't add up to anything, carelessness and guilt and recklessness and blame falling over each other, again and again, and she had no idea who had played which role in a play that had just seen its curtain in the ambulance back's glaring yellow red yellow red yellow red.

And then, without another warning, he rolled away.

Lizzie shook her head.

The ambulance went down the emptied-out stretch that went unnoticed usually, its harrowing siren bouncing between walls of glass and steel...

Without a warning, he was gone.

And so was the sense of connection that hadn't left, not even in the Wick; and not just to him.

Lizzie rushed around.

But Max was gone, too, and Sarah hadn't even bothered showing up.

Lizzie stood alone.

Around her, the fire-fighters kept gesturing hectically and the police officers turned away the curious, but no one seemed to think about turning away her.

As if she was put here for a reason.

As if she was meant to see this first hand: it was the second of the two buildings, the taller one, the one that was a little behind; Lizzie hesitated:

She looked up.

Very slowly, her eyes moved up the spine that held together this particular monster in the making.

Metre for metre.

Story for story, she moved where the glass had splintered into a massive hole. From here, where the tower's immaculate look had been destroyed so viciously, the dark smoke streamed out in a perfect plume:

From a shattered window, a black cry to an almost blue sky, so silent it was almost shy.

From here, a sign?

Lizzie almost smiled.

The steel glazed in a spring sun that was still as strong as it had been the moment she had left the Wick behind. The plume's intense black was pitched perfectly against the sky's innocent blue:

This was almost too beautiful to be real.

She closed her eyes.

From this street, a hymn to what really mattered, in the end, and that was beauty.

She pressed her eyelids together.

There was no doubt that things had calmed down: life's conflicting desires were leaning back, finally. The sun warmed her face.

Lizzie opened her eyes again.

She looked around.

In front of her, a few fire-fighters opened their visors. They stripped off their gloves and exchanged the precious reward that came with a job that was about helping others, a few deserved looks of accomplishment.

Lizzie looked away.

Soon, they would drive off.

In a few hours, all there would be left was the shattered window up there.

Soon, the police would open these artificial borders again and everything would return to normal.

Lizzie almost smiled.

Tonight, the TV cameras would deliver pictures of this very stretch into living rooms across the world and tie-wearing reporters would be speculating about motives and a so-called background, overrated and meaningless.

About relatives and friends.

And wouldn't have a clue.

The whole world would be talking about the four of them tonight.

But no one would understand a thing.

From these streets, a laugh.

The whole world would be confronted with images that only made sense to those that had been there from the beginning, two figures having been picked at random and placed on the fringe of a sweaty Shoreditch dance floor, only for four strangers to click their glasses together inside an East London pub called The George.

From these streets, a salute.

Lizzie eyed the side street that would take her away from here, beneath that small green bridge to somewhere, anywhere, stopping for a drink perhaps, finally, or perhaps not, as she collected what had to be collected: None of this made much sense yet, but whatever action was required in response to whatever had happened out here today, she felt in a good position to take it head on. She straightened herself and started walking.

This was the end.

That much was clear. Nothing else could explain the situation: the mask and the tube and the non-stop spin; Jonathan couldn't stop grinning:

This was the beginning.

He tried to push himself up a little; the strange calm that had seized his tied-up body only confirmed what he had started to suspect the moment he had started spilling the petrol up there, a match ready to be thrown:

What a bonfire!

Jonathan wanted to smile at the medic sitting next to him, but the medic didn't even give him a glance, having brand-marked him a terrorist, discarded as scum.

If only he knew what Jonathan knew.

Jonathan turned away.

If only he knew...

Jonathan stared at the white plastic ceiling; the unfamiliar peace that was flowing through his body left no doubt at all. He wanted to shout this at the medic, but this stupid mask didn't allow him to say anything:

He had done what he had done for none of the reasons he had thought he would be doing it.

The blurry notion that had driven him up the half-finished staircase, a lost love, of sorts, and a lost job, had become a very different kind of motivation the moment the flames had started spreading:

This had been about no one, but himself.

Jonathan wanted to say out loud what had dawned on him the moment the window had burst, up there:

That the crack he had inflicted on a Bishopsgate building was the kind of crack that would make his relentless search for cracks redundant, once and for all.

This had been the war to end all wars:

For the first time in his life, he had done something that would have real consequences.

For the first time ever, this was something he couldn't just walk away from.

Jonathan turned away from the ceiling.

Was anyone listening?

Surrounded by his own flames, he had finally forced responsibility upon himself. Because no one else in this world ever had.

Surrounded by his own smoke, he had finally taught himself a lesson.

Because no one out there had ever deemed that necessary.

Jonathan looked at the medic.

Why on earth were these dark green clowns speeding him through his city with their siren on?

There was nothing wrong with him!

He was a little exhausted.

That was all.

He tried to move up a little, but they had made sure he stayed where he was.

He had never felt better!

He was just a little dizzy, perhaps.

That was all.

He had never felt more alive!

He simply needed some rest. He hadn't slept properly in days, after all. He hadn't eaten. He hadn't done any of the things human beings were meant to do to keep stumbling on, but there wasn't even blood on his face, so why the alarm?

He wanted to laugh.

There was only the sweat soot from his deed, so these dark green clowns could switch off the siren and switch on the radio and find a station that would play the kind of music that would suit a scene like this...

His eyelids fell shut.

He opened them again; what he had done, he had done for everyone.

That was the magic.

His eyelids fell shut again.

He would take the blame; there was no question about that. He would stand up for what he had done.

That was the whole point.

He would plead guilty, just as he had explained to every officer out there, and that meant that all those that still needed to wake up would get their chance.

He opened his eyes again.

He would stand up for this, so that everyone would be forced to ask themselves the questions he was only asking himself right now.

His lids fell shut again.

But the darkness that came as a result was a darkness that was somehow different from the darkness Jonathan had experienced so far.

As if another force was taking over, completely, at last.

Fully, finally.

And without shame...

Jonathan tried to open his eyes again, but the lids refused to follow orders.

It remained dark.

He tried again.

But it remained dark as another force started pushing this up, finally, out of his particular mind and higher, away from the ground and into the air. Bursting the borders that had constrained everything for far too long now. Shaking off the limitations of a single perspective for a widescreen view. Zooming out, bit by bit, to provide the picture everyone must have been waiting for.

And it was getting sharper and sharper:

One like all.

All like one.

It was all coming clear, Sarah with her arms stretched on Kingsland Road, dreamily gazing into the distance.

Standing still.

And Max, on Brushfield Street now, where the sharp spire of Christ Church pierced the perfect blue sky and the sunshine made the marble look even whiter than usual.

Not moving at all.

And Lizzie, who had stopped on her walk westwards to give herself a little rest, calmly breathing in and out.

Steadily existing.

And Jonathan, inside an ambulance that was momentarily halted by an Aldgate traffic light.

It was all perfectly visible now:

One like all.

All like one.

Four fragile beings that were no more fragile than anyone else out there.

Four souls in a world, where easy guidance was out of stock, but complaining didn't help.

Four fragments, with their eyes pointed in different directions, once again.

Prepared to let go.

Ready to walk away and try again, because dark times were never an excuse.

And, as if another force insisted on directing the action, that was the picture that stayed, all four of them, standing on the streets of their city.

Looking on.

Daniel Kramb was born in 1982.
www.danielkramb.com

Acknowledgments

I would like to thank J. S. Watts for her much appreciated editorial work and feedback. For their ongoing support for this book, thanks to Rebecca Saunders and Omer Ali – this has been very important. Rebecca Omonira-Oyekanmi – thanks again for reading one of the very first drafts. Warm wishes go to Theo Visser in whose attic large parts of this book have been re-written – you are a very special person. Most of all, I would like to thank Christina Theisen – without you, there is nothing.

Lightning Source UK Ltd.
Milton Keynes UK
20 January 2011
166086UK00001B/5/P